SHADOW'S CHRISTMAS WISH

Jennifer J. Morgan

Books by Jennifer J. Morgan

Libby Madsen Cozy Mysteries

Shadows in the Forest
Spa Shadows
Shadowed Treasures
Shadow Retreats
Spooky Shadows
Shadow's Christmas Wish
The Christmas Fairy - a holiday novella

SHADOW'S CHRISTMAS WISH

Libby Madsen Cozy Mysteries, Book 6

Jennifer J. Morgan

Secret Staircase Books

Shadow's Christmas Wish
Published by Secret Staircase Books, an imprint of
Columbine Publishing Group, LLC
PO Box 416, Angel Fire, NM 87710

Book layout and design by Secret Staircase Books
First trade paperback edition: August, 2023
First e-book edition: August, 2023

Publisher's Cataloging-in-Publication Data

Morgan, Jennifer J.
Shadow's Christmas Wish / by Jennifer J. Morgan.
p. cm.
ISBN 978-1649141545 (paperback)
ISBN 978-1649141552 (e-book)

1. Libby Madsen (Fictitious character). 2. Arizona—Fiction.
3. New Mexico—Fiction. 4. Amateur sleuths—Fiction. 5. Women
sleuths—Fiction. I. Title

Libby Madsen Cozy Mystery Series : Book 6.
Morgan, Jennifer J., Libby Madsen cozy mysteries.

BISAC : FICTION / Mystery & Detective.

813/.54

To Lexi—my precious black Labrador, who crossed the Rainbow Bridge in March, 2018 at the age of 14.

I've had many precious babies over the years, but there'll never be another like you. You were right by my side during some difficult years. My constant companion, you always made me feel better no matter what I dealt with. We had incredible adventures together, too. How you loved to jump in lakes, ponds, and oceans—I still see that smile on your face when you were in water. You were a relentless hiker—you never tired, even when I was already dragging. The sweetness of your soul was so precious to me.

I'll keep your memory alive through Shadow for the rest of my life!

CHAPTER ONE

My mind kept wandering. Nearly eight weeks after our week-long haunted experience, I looked forward to the holidays and spending time with family and friends. Despite my fractured arm, I continued seeing my Ashiatsu massage clients. Using my dominant right hand, I held onto the wooden bar over my head and conducted the session with my bare feet.

Sage, my longtime client who'd become a dear friend of mine as well, asked about my injury, still wrapped up in a sling. I filled her in on the long sordid tale of our murder mystery adventures in Jerome, Arizona—real-life corpses and all. It wasn't all bad. I considered the blessings from our time there as being friendships rekindled and new ones created. I smiled, thinking about the cute bakery owners, the delicious food at the local brewery and, most of all, the time spent with my forest ranger boyfriend, Greg. Being able to see Kirby McDaniel again after so many years was icing on the cake. Everything else that occurred—hauntings, murder, and deception—not so much fun.

"Sounds like trouble follows you everywhere, Libby," Sage teased. "Hadn't you only recently found some questionable 'new friends' at that retreat near Patagonia?"

"Okay, okay. When you say it like that—" I laughed. "I guess I do meet interesting people now, don't I? Well, I wouldn't change it for anything. The good outweighs the bad, that's for sure."

She chuckled, pointedly looking at my arm again. "You're a good friend, Libby."

"Are you ready for the holidays?" I changed subjects.

"Hardly. I'm having a few girlfriends coming to visit—and I've procrastinated too long on getting my studio cleared out, so they'll have somewhere to sleep!"

Sage had the most beautiful property near the base of the Superstition Mountains east of Phoenix. I'd been there often on mobile appointments during our startup years and before we'd built the Dharma Inspired Day Spa in east Mesa. With my portable massage table set up in her casita, also her studio, I enjoyed gorgeous views and she appreciated treatment in the comfort of her own home. She also preferred a late afternoon appointment—perfect timing for some exquisite red and orange sunsets on the rocky mountain.

"Oooh, having friends staying with you for the holiday, that sounds fun. I *think*, much to my mother's chagrin, several of us are going on a ski vacation for the holiday.

Alexis, her husband JJ, and, of course, Greg."

"Things must be really going well with Greg then, yeah?"

I knew what she was getting at. I haven't ever dated a guy *this long*. That's what she really meant to say. "You know, I think so. It seems so easy. We enjoy many similar things. Yeah, I'd say it's going well. Long distance isn't easy … but after I got back from Patagonia, we both have put in the effort to travel back and forth. I mean, two hours really isn't that big of a deal."

"Not for *love*, it's not," she teased, giggling.

I dug my heel into her calf with slightly more pressure.

"Ow!" she said mockingly.

"Yeah, careful with the teasing when I'm obviously in a position of power here," I chuckled.

"So, where are you going skiing—Flagstaff?"

"No, we're headed to Taos, New Mexico, actually."

"Taos! Oh, now I'm officially jealous."

"I know, I've never been … but Greg has a former classmate that is getting married. We'll have to attend that, but otherwise, we'll have a nice long ski vacation. The Johnsons are joining us—oh, I might have already mentioned that. I'm hoping I'll be able to ski by then."

"Oh, your arm?"

"Yeah. Doctor says a couple more weeks and I should be ready. I may push that, but we'll see. I get the cast off tomorrow and start physical therapy. Since we're not actually leaving until a few days after Christmas, I should be fine. If not, I'll enjoy being a ski bunny in the lodge with a hot toddy."

Sage jumped on that. "Yeah, right. Keeping you from playing with the rest of the group? Good luck! I sense there isn't anything that keeps Libby out of the action." Her hearty laughter was infectious. Then she quieted again. "It's been several years since I've been in Taos, but you have to tell me if Sweet's Sweets is still there. Best bakery in Northern New Mexico."

Sage told me about each art gallery and restaurant in town that we need to visit. By the time we were done with her massage, I was officially famished, and ready to get to Taos. First, we'd have to survive Christmas with my family.

A couple of weeks later, I'd learn my family was nowhere near as difficult as some others.

CHAPTER TWO

My mom had outdone herself. From the decorations inside and out, to the enormous spread of food that covered the long twelve-person wooden dining table. Christmas Day was one that the Madsens always went overboard with. It all began with my late father, whom I swore competed with the neighbors every year for the best-decorated home on the block. Then Julia kept the traditions going for us kids after his tragic passing. Even now, at seventy years old, she still has that gusto to pull off the perfect holiday setting.

Greg's eyes scanned the room admiringly. He leaned over and whispered to me, "How many trees does she decorate? Does she do all this herself?"

"I've counted at least six since we walked in. I swear it's

grander every year."

He wandered away, taking in the winter wonderland. Her home was covered with little winter scenes. The Norman Rockwell-like ice skating village, Santa's workshop, the snowmen's forest, and my favorite, the near-perfect snow-covered hobbit dwellings with their tiny holiday decorated features. Each year, there are new intricate elements and my favorite thing is to find all of them before my sister, or her kids.

The holiday bells on the front door tinkled as it blew open and my nephew, Chase, bounded through. "Grandma!" he screeched, running through to the kitchen. Shadow barked and took off after Chase. All I could see was her flapping tail, and I cringed. Thankfully, I heard no crashing sounds. Yet.

I walked out the front door to see my sister, Jordan, with her hands full, struggling to get the baby out of the car seat. Pat rounded the driver's side of her large white SUV.

"Hold on. I told you I'd help. You get Ryan inside." He gently took the bags from her hands. I hurried over to help.

"Merry Christmas, Jordan," I greeted and gave her a cursory side-hug in passing. "Oh, Ryan, you're getting cuter every single day!" I patted the toddler on the head and continued to the car to help Pat and the girls.

My sister and Pat had divorced two years prior. It was a fairly amicable split, and they remained friendly for the sake of the kids. Our family always welcomed Pat to family events. I think all along we felt bad for him. He's a good guy, but honestly, never had a chance with Jordan. She's a powerhouse, and he's, well, way too nice. It wasn't surprising to me that it didn't work out. It devastated our mother. But, the way the two co-parent is admirable—we can see the kids come first, no matter what, and that's what is most important.

"Here, let me get those, Pat." I reached out and loaded up my arms with wrapped gifts. "Good to see you!"

"Merry Christmas, Libby. Has Greg joined you?"

I nodded and opened the backseat door. The twin girls were still sitting in their seats, their full attention on some YouTube video.

"Come on, girls. It's Christmas! Let's go say hi to Grandma," I coaxed.

Barely looking up, Apple mumbled, "Is Shadow here?"

"She sure is…"

Apple was the first to peel her eyes away from her screen. "Let's go, Annie … let's find Shadow."

Apple and Annie were identical; nearly nine years old now and every time I saw them, I couldn't help noticing how they seemed mature beyond their age. They were a mirror image of their mother—only with blonde hair instead of her brown.

Annie looked up, and reluctantly put her phone in the back pocket of her jeans and then they both jumped out of the vehicle and ran into the house.

"New Christmas gifts, I presume?" I asked Pat, watching them flash past.

"Yes, first iPhones. Sore subject with Jordan, I'm afraid."

We made our way inside the house, leaving gifts under the enormous tree in the living room, before heading to the kitchen with some food trays. Jordan, much like mom, always outdid herself too. She was a fantastic chef. Not professionally, but if she wanted to, she certainly could.

Instead, my sister was busy being super mom twenty-four seven. She recently launched a party planning business and was fortunate to be supported by her ex-husband's tech success.

It wasn't long before we were all seated around the dining table, passing traditional dishes. My mouth watered smelling the bubbling hot scalloped potatoes, roasted vegetables, and a spiral-cut ham. The decibel level dropped dramatically once food found its way into mouths.

"Greg, Libby says one of your friends is getting married in Taos. You're the best man?"

Greg picked up his napkin and wiped his mouth before answering.

"That's right. Best friend from college. Several of us will be there for him. Should be a great time. I haven't seen those guys in several years now."

"Yeah, I haven't heard that much about them … you'll have to get me up to speed before we get there," I mentioned.

"Where did you grow up, Greg?" Jordan interrupted.

"My parents own a ranch outside of Pagosa Springs, Colorado. I was nearly six when we moved there. Before then, we were over near Pueblo."

"Never been to either," Julia remarked before pouring another glass of wine. "Anyone else want to top off their glass?" She held the bottle up, then passed it to Jordan.

"Are you taking Shadow with you on your trip?" Apple innocently asked.

I turned to her, seeing her imploring eyes. I realized why she was asking; they were hoping to dog sit.

"Yep, we are. Alexis found a vacation rental that accepts pets. Plus, Shadow goes on all our adventures with us—she'd be sad not to."

Apple glanced at Annie. It felt like the twins were about to gang up on me. Then Chase piped up.

"But Shadow can't ski, can she?"

"No sweetie. But I don't think we'll be skiing the whole time." I held up my arm as a reminder. "I may not ski much at all. Recently got the cast off and I'll have to be careful. Shadow might have to keep me company at the ski villa if everyone else leaves me."

All the kids seemed satisfied with that explanation for now.

Pat interjected, "Will the Johnsons be joining you two? Do they even know Greg's friends?"

"Yes, Alexis, JJ, and Joshua. We're all headed to New Mexico together. There are only a couple days of obligatory wedding plans. Then, the four of us will hang out skiing, being Taos tourists, and enjoying a holiday vacation," Greg explained.

"I've got suggestions from a friend who has frequented Taos; she's recommended some restaurants and such. Alexis and I are looking forward to it," I added.

During the rest of the meal, we got caught up on everyone's news. Jordan filled us in on her new start-up business. Pat's Asian travel plans working on an extensive project he's managing sounded adventurous to me. And Mom was excited about a cruise that she and her neighbor, Margie, had recently planned—to Alaska in early summer. The kids dreaded going back to school in a couple more weeks, and Ryan was busy throwing peas off the table, watching Shadow catch them.

After clearing the table, we gathered in the living room and passed around presents. Of course, the occasion was all about the kids, so we watched them tear through all the wrappings and squeal with delight. I forgot how excited a two-year-old could get at Christmas time, and it warmed my heart. As I watched Ryan, Chase, and the twins playing as siblings do, my brain went there: *Would I ever want to have children?* I never thought so, but after meeting Greg … *Whoa, Libby! No. Not going there yet.* We were still getting to know one another. Way too soon for any of those thoughts.

Grandma, of course, spoiled each kid as she does every single year. She also spoiled us adults. My mother can be overbearing at times, but she has a heart of gold and has always been exceedingly generous. This year was no exception. It shocked Greg when she handed him a present.

"Julia, you shouldn't have …" he blushed.

"Greg, you are every bit a part of this family now, too," she smiled.

"Aww, thank you so much." He carefully opened the exquisitely wrapped box. That's another thing my mother is great at. She must have worked in a gift wrap department at some point—I've never been as good at it as she. "Julia, how did you know?" He looked directly at me and I shrugged.

"Well, Santa told me, of course," she chuckled. "Hopefully, you can use them in your truck."

He pulled out two new black Weather Tech floor mats that read *Tundra* in red lettering on the side of each one. "These are perfect! Thank you!"

Pat opened a beautiful black leather backpack style laptop bag monogrammed with his initials. He peered into each of the zippered compartments. "Julia, you've done too much. Thank you for this—it's going to work so well.

I really appreciate it."

After everyone had finished opening their gifts, I sat back, admiring the melee. Wrappings were *everywhere*. Shadow couldn't help herself; she nosed her way and scampered through, getting friskier with the sound of rustling paper. The kids got in on the action, wadding up paper and throwing it into the air and watching Shadow jump up to catch, then rip them into shreds.

Later that evening, I couldn't help but think what a perfect Christmas day it'd been, as we packed the 4Runner up with our new treasures, leftovers, and an exhausted dog.

"Thanks, Mom." I wrapped my arms around and squeezed her tight. "Thank you for everything."

"Now, you be careful driving on those snowy roads. I'm not sure about all this." Her pursed lips slowly morphed into a broad smile. "But, have fun. I know how you like your adventures." She kissed my cheek and pulled away to give Greg the same spiel.

Jordan grabbed my arm before I could climb into the vehicle. "Let's get together when you get back. You're always busy with your little business—feels like I haven't seen you in months. Would be good to spend a girl's day together, wouldn't it?"

"Yep," I said, noncommittally. "You're right; it's been a while." I hugged her and climbed into the passenger seat. I hadn't even let her belittling comment about my business get to me.

Later that evening, after Greg had left for home and all was quiet, I poured a cup of tea and snuggled up on the sofa with Shadow. That was when I realized I hadn't stopped smiling from the time I'd walked in the door earlier. What a special Christmas Day with my family. As I sipped my tea, the tingle in my belly spread upwards, causing an even larger smile on my face. Greg was part of my family now.

My wishes have been answered, I thought to myself as I rubbed Shadow's head. She stretched her body and leaned into the mini-massage. "What is your special Christmas wish, sweet girl?" I whispered to her. She opened her eyes and let out a groan. "Oh, yeah. That's all? Nothing but a massage now and then? You are easy to shop for then." I giggled.

CHAPTER THREE

Our time apart was short-lived. Several days later, we left for our ski vacation. During our eight-hour trip to Albuquerque, I found myself staring at Greg during conversation. He certainly was handsome—I realized how much he looked like that hunky actor, Chris Hemsworth. Tall, muscular, short brown wavy hair, crystal blue eyes, and a chiseled scruffy jawline. *How had I gotten so lucky?* Not only was he gorgeous, he was simply a nice guy.

The entire journey passed quickly; we shared driving time in my 4Runner and it went seamlessly. I don't think we stopped talking the entire way. I wanted to know all about Greg's friends and their college days. Mainly, I wanted to know what I was stepping into, agreeing to attend this wedding.

I learned that the groom, Peter Schull, was one of three roommates of Greg's during his college years at New Mexico State University in Las Cruces. Peter was the most precocious, and I was told the stories about him were endless. Michael Thorn and Neeraj Prasad were the other two roommates. They shared a large house for several years. It sounded as though they got into their fair share of typical college student shenanigans—I made a mental note to pry and learn more later. For now, he informed me that Peter and Neeraj were business majors, and Michael was a mechanical engineer. Greg was the odd man out, studying agriculture. There was another guy they worked with, Hector Salazar, who was part of the wedding party, but Greg hadn't ever met him.

By the time graduation rolled around, Michael had engineered a new state-of-the-art medical device. Peter, being the slick and natural salesperson, found investors and the two went into business together. The company was called MedDyno Industries—Michael was the Chief Executive and Innovation Officer. Peter, President of Global Sales. Neeraj, being a whiz with finance, also joined them as their Chief Financial Officer. All three of them grew the medical device conglomerate, achieving tremendous success. Again, Greg went his own direction, breaking from the pack.

"Did you ever wish you'd joined them, too?" I asked.

"No! No, I belong outdoors. They were always the studious business and engineer types. I would be miserable doing what they do."

I laughed, thinking about Greg all buttoned up in a business suit each day, sitting at a desk behind a computer. No, he was right; not at all his personality.

"So, this wedding is going to be a huge affair, isn't it?"

He glanced over. "Probably. Yes. They don't do anything halfway. I'm sure it's going to have all the glitz and glamor. Although it is in the mountains at a ski resort—maybe they've found their outdoorsy personalities after all?" He chuckled at the thought.

"And what about the bride?"

"I've never met her."

"So, they didn't meet in college or anything, then?"

"No. All he's really told me is they've been dating for close to two years. Oh, I guess he mentioned he met her at a charity event and they hit it off. I don't really know much more than that since I haven't seen him, or any of them, for so many years. Once I moved to Arizona, and got caught up in my forestry job, we lost touch, other than maybe a few calls a year. I hope we'll get to catch up on this trip, but you know how it is at a wedding—lots of people around."

We were approaching the west side of Albuquerque on I-40, and I glanced in the side mirror. The other SUV in our caravan followed safely behind. It was almost as though Alexis had read my mind; the two-way radio squawked, and I picked it up. As Alexis talked, I could hear Joshua's small five-year-old voice in the background asking to talk to Auntie Libby.

"Joshua, are you enjoying the long car ride?" I asked playfully.

He got quiet. "Um. I fell asleep."

We laughed. "Are you ready to go see snow?"

"Yes!" he hollered.

"Would it be okay if I talked to your mommy now?"

"I guess." We heard a lot of shuffling and, "Here, Mom!"

Alexis was still laughing as she talked into the radio. "He's wide awake now. We're following you to the hotel, right?"

"Yes, the one just off I-40 … we'll take the Carlisle exit."

"10-4."

"Hey, what's the plan for tonight?" JJ hollered into the radio.

"Greg has best man duties—final tuxedo fitting and pickup, and evening plans—I thought we'd settle in at the hotel and then go find some dinner. Anything in particular you'd like to do in Albuquerque?"

"Nope, sounds great! I'm so excited to get to Taos tomorrow."

"Us too!"

We pulled up to the hotel, got checked in, and took Shadow for a short walk around the property. The place was an extended-stay hotel, almost an apartment-like setting—many two-story buildings, all with several units each. Joshua joined Shadow and me; the kid was so wound up after being in a car for nearly eight hours. He ran up and down the sidewalks, between buildings, and back again. It drove Shadow crazy; she wanted off her leash to run freely with her little buddy.

Eventually, we found our way back to his parents in their room; I left him to go find Greg in ours.

"Oh, this is a nice place. Too bad we're not staying longer," I commented, walking around, seeing for the first time that we had a two-story little apartment. There was a small living room and kitchen arrangement downstairs, and a bedroom and bathroom combination upstairs.

"Yeah, but wait until you see the house they provided

us in Taos. Right near the ski runs; looks amazing online."

I reached my arms around Greg, giving a giant hug. "I cannot wait! This is going to be so much fun." My lips found his and lingered there, enjoying his kiss. "So, what's the plan for tonight? When are you leaving us?"

He checked his watch; it was nearly four o'clock. "Looks like I've got to giddy up. I'm heading uptown and need to meet everyone at four-thirty. I honestly don't know what time I'll be back tonight." His brows furrowed. "I'm sorry. I feel bad leaving you and our friends like this."

"No, no. It's been the plan—it's okay! Tonight, and tomorrow night, then the wedding and you're done. Then, we'll get you to ourselves again for the rest of the week."

"Yes, promise. Only a couple of days, then we'll enjoy our ski vacation with no time constraints or other obligations." He leaned over; his kiss left me wanting more. "Ugh, I don't want to leave." He pulled away and rushed around, looking for the keys and his wallet before turning back to me. "What are you and the Johnsons going to do?"

"We'll find some dinner, but I think we're all pooped and will probably hit the sack early and be raring to go in the morning."

Another kiss as he breezed by to the door, then he was gone. For several seconds, a strange feeling swept over me. *No, he'll be okay. Everything will be okay.*

There was a knock on the door and I dashed to open it quickly, thinking he must have forgotten something. I opened the door, and instead, found Alexis standing there. Her smile radiant and infectious; her tawny skin glowing, and clearly happy to be on vacation. She immediately brought a huge smile to my face.

"Oh, hi! Come on in. Greg just left."

Her large brown eyes took in the room. "Yours is similar to ours. You don't have a bedroom down here, though."

"No, we only have one."

"I think the crew is hungry. Wanna grab dinner early?"

Whole-heartedly agreeing, we settled on a highly recommended New Mexican restaurant off Fourth Street. I got Shadow settled into her kennel and we headed out.

The dinner recommendation from Sasha was spot-on. We shared tastes of several traditional Spanish and Native American-inspired delicacies: calabacitas, green-chile chicken stuffed sopapillas, and red stacked enchiladas topped with a fried egg. It wasn't long before we found our bellies satiated and ready for a nice, long sleep.

* * *

SLAM!

Shadow barked.

I jolted up in bed, trying to get my bearings. The time on the bedside clock said it was shortly before three. My hand reached to my left, brushing along covers. Greg wasn't in bed and then I remembered he had gone out with his friends. *Hours ago…*

Pounding sounded again; my heart leaped. It wasn't my imagination; I had heard something. Quickly, I got out of bed and pulled on sweatpants, grabbed my cell phone, and quietly navigated the stairs to the first-floor living room. I let Shadow out of her crate and shushed her. She ran for the front door.

The only light in the room shone from the electronics on the TV stand. I gently approached the front door and peered out the peephole, expecting to see Greg, who must have lost his key card. My pulse quickened and I looked from side to side; no one was in sight. *Maybe it was someone knocking on another door?* Shadow nudged me and I reached down to reassure her.

I moved over to the sofa and sat, trying to calm down. Shadow followed and sat on my feet, staring at me as though she had the same question. *Where was Greg?* Rubbing my eyes to clear the cobwebs of sleep, I looked at the cell phone I'd been clutching onto. One message from Greg showed it came in around eleven.

Late night. Don't wait up.

That was four hours ago.

We sat in the dark for several more minutes, listening intently. It was quiet, other than some freeway noise in the distance. I headed back to bed and allowed Shadow to join me; Greg wasn't locked out, and the pounding must have come from the neighboring unit. She settled on the floor right next to the bed.

Finally settling down again, and after what felt like hours, I dozed off. There it was again—a loud crash. I sat straight up. Shadow bolted down the stairs.

Whatever I heard was close, and this time I was sure it wasn't a noise from next door. I frantically looked around. There was nothing close by to use as a weapon, but I grabbed my phone. As soon as the screen light shone, I saw Greg's form in the doorway.

"Sorry. I was really trying to be quiet…" he whispered.

I turned on the light and we both grimaced, squinting to adjust to it.

"You scared the heck out of me!"

"I'm so sorry, hon."

I checked the time—four-thirty.

He looked embarrassed as he rounded the bed, taking off his clothes, and peeling back the covers.

"Did you try to get in the door a couple of hours ago?" I asked.

He shook his head. "No, Hector dropped me off a few minutes ago."

"Where'd you leave my 4Runner then?"

"Yeah, sorry about that. Had one too many. Don't worry, it's at Pete's house … I'll need JJ to take me over there to get it before we head out."

"Thanks for not driving. But, really … we're leaving here in a matter of hours and you're drunk!"

"I know. I know. It's been so long since I've seen the guys, though. Oh, man … I need sleep. What time do we have to leave?"

Irritated beyond belief, I couldn't answer his question. I simply turned out the light, laid down, and rolled away from him. His snoring began as soon as his head hit the pillow. My mind raced a thousand miles a minute, wondering where they'd been all night. I hadn't even met the friends, and they kept Greg out until the wee hours of the morning on the first night we arrived. At least he was safe, I kept telling myself.

After another thirty minutes, I decided I wasn't getting any more sleep. I got up and made coffee, making no effort to be quiet. Nothing roused the late-night partier, so I grabbed Shadow's harness, which we call her 'bra', snapped on her leash, and went outside for a walk.

Albuquerque in the winter months is quite cold, I discovered. Far more than where I live in Mesa, Arizona. Bundled in my down jacket, a scarf around my neck and pulled over my nose, I wondered if Shadow should have some covering too. I hadn't even thought of that previously, but later today we'd be going to a much higher elevation. If this was cold, that was going to get even more interesting. We wound our way along paths through the hotel's property and ended up on a larger city street. At this hour, there was little traffic, and the sun had barely lightened the top of the Sandia Mountains. It felt colder as we walked and I wished I'd remembered my knit cap to cover my head.

I couldn't stop the thoughts running through my head. For the first time in nearly nine months, I felt angry with Greg. Since when was he the type who stayed out all night getting drunk? I'd barely seen him have one, maybe two, drinks at any function we'd attended together. I hadn't seen this side to him before. Why did it bother me so much? I mean, when I get together with old friends … uh, no, I'm pretty much the same old Libby. Sure, I have a drink or two in social situations, but I can't honestly remember a time I've actually been drunk. And that doesn't count the time at that retreat during the fall when someone drugged me—I *hadn't* chosen that. Ugh. That memory was one I liked to keep in the past.

As we rounded the corner to head back to the hotel, I could feel the cobwebs breaking free in my brain. Fresh air was definitely the remedy to a lack of sleep and waking up grumpy. Shadow helped sniff our way back to our apartment door. I felt my phone vibrate in my pocket when I reached for the key card.

"Good morning, Lexi," I answered.

"The boys are eager to get to the snow. Do we have an estimated departure?" she laughed.

"Wow! You guys are up early."

"Oh shoot, did we wake you guys?"

"No. Shadow and I are out for a walk. Greg's sleeping off his alcohol induced night."

"Oooh, he tied one on, huh?"

"Oh yeah. Got in after four this morning."

"Oh, jeez!" she gasped.

"Yeah, guess I'm driving today. Speaking of which, can you guys give me a lift to my car … he left it at his friend's place."

"Sure. Maybe we go do that, grab some breakfast, and let him sleep."

"Sounds like a plan. Give me half an hour to get cleaned up and try to wrangle an address from him."

"See you then."

* * *

We pulled up to an upscale neighborhood called Sandia Heights. Although I couldn't get a coherent answer from Greg, he pointed me to where he'd stored the address in his phone and we Googled it. As we rounded the last corner to Peter's house, my jaw dropped. The place was enormous—a mansion. There was a lengthy lane that led to a circular drive; it looked like a luxury car lot. BMWs, Cadillac, Lexus, Lamborghini, Jaguar—you name it, and there it was. At the apex of the circle, I saw my Trina. Yes, I name my cars—this Toyota became Trina. She looked lonely and out of place amongst the sportier looking models. But I was proud of her—she was the most reliable vehicle I've ever owned. Who cares about the labels of the richy-rich?

"Okay, guys … thanks for the ride. I'll meet you over at the restaurant." I hopped out of their Lexus.

We'd passed a place called Wecks. From their Yelp reviews, that was my vote and the Johnsons agreed. Walking into the restaurant, it looked like an ordinary diner. Once our food arrived, we agreed with the great reviews. JJ devoured the huevos rancheros, Alexis chose a chorizo breakfast burrito smothered in a delicious red sauce, and I opted for a veggie omelet. It was Joshua's testament to a sumptuous meal that sealed the deal for us. He was silent for the entire time, captivated by his stack of chocolate chip pancakes and bacon. When he finally looked around the table, the scene was classic. His face was completely blanketed in chocolate. I couldn't help breaking out laughing. I grabbed my phone as quickly as I could and snapped the photo.

It was still early, around eight o'clock, by the time we made it back to the hotel. I began packing stuff up in Trina as quietly as I could, deciding that we'd be ready once Greg slept it off. Around ten, he finally stirred. I brought him a cup of coffee and a breakfast burrito we'd ordered as takeout; his complexion turned shades of green when he caught the aroma. He ran to the bathroom.

"This is going to be a fun ride up a winding mountain road, isn't it?" I hollered. The sounds coming from behind the door indicated my comment didn't make his situation any better.

By checkout time, we finally got him out the door. The color had come back into his cheeks; the food helped soak up the night's debauchery, and we started the two-hour drive north on I-25.

"I can't believe those guys," he spoke softly. "I mean,

we used to party it up in college, sure. But they apparently have kept up their tolerance for it."

"Where'd you guys go?"

"Oh, man … it started out as a pool party at Peter's house late afternoon. He has a personal chef. Can you believe that? There was food galore and the drinks kept pouring. Then, a party bus showed up. I mean, it really was like a fancy van of sorts. The driver took us to one of his clubs."

"*His* clubs?" I asked. "I thought he was in medical sales."

"Yes, he owns several clubs in town. Both gentlemen's establishments," he winked, "and dance clubs."

"You went dancing?"

"I didn't dance, but yes, we visited each of his clubs. I swear the whole evening was about him showing off everything he owns. How well established he is in Albuquerque and how successful he is. It was kind of weird, actually."

"It surprised me how late you were out."

"I know. I'm really sorry about that. I wanted to come home much earlier, but I am the best man … and, well…"

"No, I get it. Did you have fun, though?"

"Well, feeling the way I do now … definitely wasn't worth it. But, yes, I enjoyed the time with my buddies. It's been so long and that part was fun."

"What part wasn't?"

"It's hard feeling adequate around that group. I mean, with all they've accomplished already. It's insane."

"You do important work too, Greg," I added.

"Yeah. I know." He rested his head back, putting his hands on his stomach. "How much farther?"

"More than an hour." I glanced over at him. "Do you need to stop?"

"Nah. Just rest."

"So, I assume since the wedding's tomorrow that there is some sort of plan for tonight?"

"Ugh. Yes. The rehearsal dinner."

"And I'm joining you for that, right?"

He rolled his head toward me. "Yes. Is that okay?"

"Of course. Plus, then you can use me as the excuse when we need to leave before midnight," I smiled, reached over and squeezed his hand.

* * *

Pulling up to our vacation rental, I turned to Greg.

"How much did you say this cost us? It's pretty fancy …" I parked in front of the three-bay garage structure and JJ parked right next to us.

"We didn't. Peter has paid for everything."

"What? I guess I hadn't realized that. For the entire week, or only this weekend?"

He pulled out the paperwork from the glove compartment.

"We need this for the lock box code on the door." He read through some instructions, flipped the page, then said, "Yep, looks like all week long. Everything's prepaid."

"Holy cow! This is nice."

We both climbed out of the car and let Shadow out. The remote acreage was in the Taos Ski Valley, which backed up to the forest and the ski resort. Alexis and her family walked over to us and we all stood staring at the gigantic pitched-roof mansion.

My tall, blonde detective friend stood staring straight ahead with his mouth open. "Um, guys … how much do we owe you for our share?" JJ hesitantly asked.

"Nothing."

"There's no way we could all afford something like this," Alexis stated, pointing toward the gorgeous home.

"The bride and groom have put all of us up in vacation rentals," Greg answered. "Don't worry, after what I saw last night—this is a pittance to them."

We started toward the front door. Greg punched in the code and opened the enormous wooden carved front door. The carvings illustrated forested trees, a large bear, some elk in the distance, and flying eagles.

"This door costs more than I earn in a year," JJ commented as we all walked through the threshold. "Whoa!" He looked up at the high ceilings, surveying the two thousand square feet of living and kitchen area, filled with brown and tan leather furniture. There were several seating arrangements, from expansive sectional sofas to reclining chairs and settees. Various animal trophy heads hung from the walls and there were enormous elk horn chandeliers hanging from the ceiling.

Alexis and I dashed immediately to the spectacular kitchen. The Viking gas stove, Jenn Air wall ovens (yes, plural), and a massive Sub-Zero refrigerator. It was the dream of every chef—top-notch appliances and plenty of space.

Shadow followed us all around the place, checking every corner. The place was built along a sloping hillside with a terraced landscape. The ground level we previously had walked into was the main floor. From there, two wings of the house were built into the hillside. We started by checking out the downstairs level to our right. We took the stairs, but observed an elevator available as well. When we arrived at the bottom of the landing, we found an entire floor, which appeared to be a completely separate apartment. This section was also two-story, as it continued the graduation on the hillside. Alexis and JJ chose to stay here. It had three bedrooms, one of which the owner had set up as a playroom. Joshua was already checking out the TV and gaming system. He looked our direction before we walked out. His wide smile and sparkling deep brown eyes made the small child's golden complexion glow with excitement.

"Well, that'll keep him plenty busy," JJ said.

We left him there while we explored the rest of the Johnson's floor, then we made our way over to the left wing of the home. Both wings of the house were identical architecturally, each residence similar, except the left wing comprised two bedrooms instead of three. The spacious primary suites in each wing had to be over a thousand square feet each. We were sufficiently impressed, admiring the sitting room, in addition to the bedroom with a fireplace. The extensive bathroom, with state-of-the-art showers and jetted spas, and closets that were the size of most children's bedrooms. I'd seen nothing like this before—it was too much.

"We're going to be lost in this place, I'm sure of it." I opened and closed doors, amazed at everything. "Who rents out a place this grand?"

Greg opened up the patio door. "Guys, check this out."

We walked out onto a substantial patio. They had cleared the snow from it; there was a grill and tables, a sizable hot tub that appeared to hold ten or more people, and around the outer edges of the patio, there was fencing and a gate. We ventured that way and Shadow jumped in a pile of snow and started darting all around, spraying snow everywhere.

"She's in her element," I laughed.

"Look, there are ski tracks. It's a pathway."

Greg opened the gate, cautious not to let Shadow out of the fenced area. He walked out several feet into the trees. "Yep, he said it was close enough to the ski hills. I couldn't figure out how from the directions driving in, but here's the answer..." he said, coming back through the gate.

Sure enough, we could ski right off the patio. Through the trees where Greg pointed, we now saw several people whiz by on a nearby run.

Alexis stood with her mouth wide open. "We never even looked at the patio on the other side. Maybe that has access also?"

I stared all around at everything, taking it in. "This is all too much. I would have been perfectly fine with a little two-bedroom cabin, honestly." I wondered what type of dinner rehearsal I was walking into tonight. *Had I brought appropriate wedding attire?*

JJ walked up to Greg, gave him a slap on his back. "I think we're going to like your friends!" They both laughed. "Brrrr ... let's get back inside and settle in."

We unloaded both cars and everyone went their own directions, getting unpacked, before meeting up again in the living room on the main floor. Once we could peel Joshua away from the playroom, we drove into Taos to pick up some groceries and scope out the town.

CHAPTER FOUR

Greg offered his arm, steadying me as we climbed the stairs to Peter's front door. High heels have never been my thing, but then add in winter snow-packed sidewalks. There really should be a law about this. You know, for safety's sake. If men had to walk five steps unbalanced, wearing these potential ankle twisters, they wouldn't exist at all.

A handsome man in a tuxedo answered the door and welcomed us to the Schull household. Nearly the second we walked in, they presented a tray of champagne glasses to us. I accepted. Greg declined. He still appeared green around the edges; I chuckled to myself.

Glancing around the room, taking in all the elegantly dressed people, I was grateful Alexis had pulled me into the quaint boutique in Taos earlier. The little black dress I'd originally packed would not have cut it in this crowd. She had helped me pick out a trendy A-line deep cobalt velvet dress with a hem about mid-calf length and a black faux fur stole. However, the matching stilettos were a bit much in my opinion. I already felt the urge to take them off and go barefoot. I guessed that wouldn't be appropriate, though.

My eyes caught a tall, muscular man, his black crew cut peppered with silver, and a model-like brilliant smile who was swiftly heading our direction.

"You must be Libby!" His bright green eyes held onto mine as he reached out to shake my hand. He looked at Greg. "You did not warn me how beautiful your girlfriend is, my man."

I blushed. Greg pulled me closer to his side.

"Libby, this is the one and only, Peter Schull. Peter, yes, this is *my* gorgeous girlfriend, Libby Madsen."

"The pleasure is all mine," Peter cooed. "Please, come meet my wife-to-be." He pushed through the crowd, heading toward the blazing fireplace, and we followed.

"Tammi!" he hollered over the music. "You have to meet Greg and Libby!"

A platinum blonde, petite woman, wearing a cream-colored long silk dress that clung to her lean body, twisted around at the sound of Peter's voice. She had her hair tied back in a neat chignon at the bottom of her neck. Her long bangs draped over most of her forehead, softening her sharp, angular facial features. The dazzling smile matched that of her fiancé's and I immediately figured out what brought the two together. They were model-perfect people, living a millionaire-perfect life.

I felt Greg tense as she approached. Curious, I glanced

at him before she reached us. His face turned ashen.

"Greg!" she reached out a delicate hand. "So nice to *meet* you." The sparkle of her deep brown eyes met his with anticipation. I observed Greg quickly shake her hand, never making eye contact. Sweat appeared on his brow.

She then turned to me. "Libby. Welcome," she said, with much less enthusiasm, but polite all the same. I smiled and greeted her, commenting on what a lovely place they had.

Greg broke the momentary awkward pause by excusing himself, asking where the restroom was. He left me with the soon-to-be-married couple I'd only barely met. Startled by his behavior, I wondered if he really was feeling poorly from last night. The way his hands got all clammy and his face turned gray, that must be the reason. Poor guy.

"So, Libby … tell me, what do you do for a living? Are you into forestry work as well?" she asked me.

"Oh, no. I am a massage therapist in Mesa. I am the co-owner of Dharma Inspired Day Spa."

"How lovely! Greg's a lucky guy," she winked. "Having a *therapist* around." She and Peter had a good chuckle over that.

"Hey, Libby …" Peter started, reaching his arm up and signaling someone from across the room. "There are Greg's parents now!"

Greg's parents are here? He never mentioned that.

I whipped around and saw a couple crossing the room. They were both tall and fit; she had short auburn hair, and he had brownish gray hair. My mind went into a tailspin, trying to remember. *What had he told me about his parents?* Very little.

Peter saw my discomfort. "You haven't met his parents yet?"

I shook my head.

"Peter! How the heck are you doing, son?" He shook hands with Peter and then waved his arm around, admiring their home. "It looks like you are doing very well for yourself, indeed."

The woman moved forward and hugged Peter. "So good to see you after all these years. You look well! And where the heck is *my son*? We've been looking…"

"Gene. Betsy. I'd like you both to meet Libby Madsen!"

No recognition, but they each moved forward and politely shook my hand. Then Betsy softly asked, "Are you here for the bride or groom?"

Peter looked confused. "Oh, Betsy. Gene. This is Greg's girlfriend!"

Awkward. I wanted to slink away. Instead, I smiled. *Where was Greg? Had he never even mentioned my name to his parents?*

Greg's father was the first to speak. "Oh, Libby … how nice to meet you," he repeated politely.

The smug expression from Tammi, taking a sip of champagne, hanging back watching the entire episode, was too much. Then, I put it together. *Greg doesn't know they invited his parents. Why?*

Greg cautiously approached our group.

"Mom?" he questioned, then hugged her. "Dad?" They shook hands and his dad pulled him in for a hug and back slap. "I had no idea you were coming to the wedding! Why didn't you tell me?"

Peter laughed heartily and pulled Tammi closer to his side. "Surprise!"

I watched as everyone laughed. Everyone but Tammi, who continued her unnerving smirk. Her reaction wasn't joy over the family reunion necessarily. She appeared to be thrilled by the deception. *What was her story?*

Greg looked at me apologetically. "Sorry, Libby … I did not know they were coming. Really."

I smiled and nodded. No need to get into that now.

Betsy reached out and touched Tammi on the arm, "And it's so nice seeing you again, Tammi!" She leaned over and kissed her cheek.

Tammi's eyes found Greg's, before responding to Betsy. "Yes. And I'm so honored you're here. After all, I've always thought of you as Mom."

Greg nearly choked on his water.

Peter looked confused. "You know Greg's parents?" he asked Tammi.

"Oh honey, don't you remember … I told you that Greg and I dated back in high school? In Pueblo. Old, old history," she scoffed, waving him off.

Betsy, Gene, and Tammi were the only ones not bothered by the revelation. My mouth stood gaping. Greg flushed a hundred shades of red. And Peter's never-ending smile came to an abrupt halt.

"Dude," Peter turned to Greg. "Why didn't you tell me?"

"I did not know! You mentioned your fiancée's name was Tammi, but you never shared a picture or anything about her. How was I to know?"

"Last name on the wedding invitation?" he spat.

"I didn't recognize it," Greg defended, looking over at me with pleading eyes.

"Ok, then … how about when I introduced you two … not even ten minutes ago?" Peter questioned loudly. The bustling crowd around us seemed to go quiet. All eyes were on our group.

"Okay guys," Tammi interjected. "That was ancient history. We're here to have fun—we can reminisce later. Come on, let's crank up that music!" she yelled out, with arms in the air, dancing her way through the crowd.

Whoever was in charge of the music certainly did as they were told. The music blared and everyone went back to dancing and trying to talk over the noise.

Greg and Peter moved their conversation outside on the back patio.

I set my empty champagne glass down and went in search of a restroom.

CHAPTER FIVE

After catching my breath in their luxurious bathroom for who knows how long, I regained my composure and ventured out into the party crowd again. I walked through the enormous residence admiring features that only super wealthy people enjoy. The artwork, sculptures, antiques … all of it smelled of money.

A portion of the expansive living area was now an impromptu dance floor; its centerpiece was Tammi. Dancing, whooping, hollering, everyone was having a great time. As I made my way through throngs of people, I finally found a buffet in the dining area just past the kitchen. That's right, this was called a rehearsal dinner, yet no one had mentioned food since we'd arrived. I hardly felt hungry, but scoped out the offerings, anyway. At least, it seemed to be the least crowded area of the house at the moment.

Inside the dining room, I found the buffet setup. Carving stations—roasted chicken, prime rib, and brisket—along with a long line of steaming hot dishes. Reading the description cards, there were many delicious options: gorgonzola scalloped potatoes, steamed asparagus, bacon-wrapped scallops, and those were only the ones nearest me. I looked farther down and that's when I saw that the Lawsons were in line, filling their plates as well.

"Libby, please … join us. We seem to have lost our son again." Gene extended the invite.

Not wanting to be rude, I graciously accepted and put a few items on a plate. When I joined them at their table, I recognized Greg's brother and sister from a photo I'd seen at his house once.

"Libby, these are Greg's siblings—Dana and Larry. Kids, this is Greg's girlfriend, Libby." We all shook hands before I took the seat that Larry pulled out for me, right next to him.

"Great to meet you all, finally," I said, unrolling my black cloth napkin. I noticed the elegant burgundy-colored monogrammed 'S'. I smoothed it out in my lap before making eye contact with Larry, who'd watched every movement I'd made so far. He smiled widely, staring uncomfortably at me.

"So nice to meet you, too," Dana said, bringing my attention back to the table. I suspected she also knew nothing prior about Greg and I dating. "How long have you guys been together?"

"Let's see, it's been around nine months."

I saw Betsy and Dana flinch at my answer.

"Nine months!" Larry said aloud, then chuckled. He picked up his beer, chugging half of it down.

"How'd you guys meet?" Gene asked.

I finally addressed the situation politely. "He hasn't told you a thing about me, has he?"

They all shook their heads.

"Well, we met at a campground near where he lives. He assisted with the search and rescue of a girl—daughter of a client of mine—early last summer."

"A client? What do you do for a living?" Gene asked.

"I'm a massage therapist." I slowed at the audible gasp from Betsy. *Had Larry actually bumped his chair over closer to mine?* I wondered, giving him a side glance. "I own Dharma Inspired Day Spa—co-owner with my best friend, Alexis. He hasn't told you any of this?"

In unison, all four heads moved slowly, showing me the answer. No.

"Well, I'm sorry about that. I guess we hadn't discussed the whole 'meet the parents' thing yet..." I started nervously. Although, images flashed of the time he'd met my mother—*months* earlier.

"Has he met yours?" Dana asked.

I nodded my head, knowing that another gasp was imminent from Betsy. She didn't let me down.

"Umm, yes, he has met my mom and sister. My dad, unfortunately, passed away when I was sixteen."

Dana and Betsy exchanged glances when they thought I wasn't looking. Gene solemnly offered his apologies about my deceased father.

Larry swallowed a mouthful of brisket before he turned to me. "And about massage ..."

Gene cleared his throat, giving the eager young man

a pointed look. "Son, I'm sure Libby doesn't want to talk about work while on vacation."

For the rest of our time at the dinner table, I enjoyed learning more about Greg's family. I knew the basics—they lived in Pagosa Springs, Colorado. Average conservative middle-income family: she had always played the role of housewife, taking care of the home and family. Earlier in his career, he was an insurance adjuster while their kids were younger and living in Pueblo, Colorado. Since that time, he'd inherited his father's cattle ranch near Pagosa Springs, and that's what he has continued to do full time.

Greg's sister, Dana Birch, is married with two kids, a boy who's eight and a girl aged ten. Dana's an accountant for a large real estate company. I got the idea her mother didn't understand why she had to work outside the home. Of course, maybe I read that situation incorrectly, I don't know. Dana's husband, Joe, worked as a commercial airline pilot and that's why he wasn't with them on this trip. He was on call for the busy holiday period. I asked about her kids—they were back at the rental home Peter had arranged for the family—he'd also arranged for a nanny.

It was no surprise to me when Larry began talking about his career of doing odd-jobs, and mostly seasonal work. He'd been a ski and surfing instructor for most of his adult life, but also guided white water rafting expeditions as well. That fit along with his long bleach-blonde locks, trim physique, and casual attitude. I easily pictured how he was finding his purpose. I suspected that included quite the menagerie of women as well.

They were a lovely family; and once we'd learned more about one another, I felt much more comfortable. I still couldn't understand why Greg hadn't spoken much about them or why he hadn't mentioned me to them. Nine months into our relationship, and having already met my family, I only assumed that would be the natural order of things. I hadn't gotten feelings from the family that there was any bad blood amongst them. They all appeared to get along great. Of course, there were the few obviously apparent, typical family quirks, but they seemed close. It also appeared Greg hadn't opened up about his life in Arizona. There was much they didn't know about his job and where he was living.

I asked about Tammi and I got an earful about the story of the football player and cheerleader love story of the nineties. It shocked me to hear the story. It's not that Greg and I routinely talked about past relationships, but one of such significance, and as his family portrayed, should have had a mere mention. Of course, I hadn't told him about my high school romance either. But, in that case, what was there to tell?

Greg's high school love sounded different to me. To listen to his family, they were certain that the two would marry and have several young ones. *That* sounded serious to me. It definitely explained why Greg turned an ashen gray when he saw her. Guess it wasn't last night's debauchery, after all. And Peter didn't know about Greg dating Tammi? I had a hard time believing that. Hadn't Betsy mentioned visiting with Tammi frequently since the *kids* graduated? Tammi would come over for coffee whenever she was in the area.

Dana told me how Tammi moved away from Pagosa several times over the years—most likely for various relationships, I guessed. Dana mentioned it surprised them when they got the wedding invitation, but that was Tammi.

Popping in and out of their lives. Had Greg known how close she'd stayed with his family? Was that why he hadn't mentioned me? I was so confused.

As we finished a sampling of exquisitely designed desserts, the bride summoned everyone to the great room. I scanned the room, looking for Greg and Peter, but didn't see them. Tammi took a microphone, stood on a rectangular stone coffee table, motioned to the DJ to turn down the music, quieting the raucous crowd.

"Has anyone seen my future husband?" she called out, giggling. "Anyone?"

Everyone began glancing around. No one spoke up.

"Anyone see his best man?" she hollered. "C'mon Betsy, Gene … where are you hiding that son of yours?" Tammi stumbled slightly, then laughed it off, as those around her gasped, reaching for her. Betsy and Gene shrugged their shoulders. "Okay. Well, then. No speeches tonight! We'll save that for tomorrow night instead when I'm Mrs. Peter SCHULL!" she enunciated her new moniker loudly.

A girl, who I presumed might be Tammi's best friend, held her hand out for the bride-to-be and helped her off the table. Then she took the microphone from Tammi and continued the loud spiel.

"Hi y'all! Don't forget, skiing tomorrow morning! Yep, it's the bride and groom's favorite activity, so that's how we're starting our day. Please join us at eight; we'll meet at the base of the gondola lift, and you don't want to miss out!" she held up a champagne glass as though she expected us to toast to that.

"Oh! And remember to check the wedding weekend itinerary when you're back at your places—this party is only the beg-inn-ing of a super fun-filled weekend. All day *and* night tomorrow will be a PARTY —before *and* after the wedding ceremony!" she screeched. "Oh, and it all wraps up with a beautiful brunch and more skiing on Sunday. Enjoy yourselves!"

She set the microphone on the table without turning it off, subjecting us to the horrendous feedback. Someone grabbed it and turned it off as the music cranked up and everyone began dancing again.

Tammi sure wasn't concerned about her fiancé's absence. I was getting anxious about where Greg disappeared to; it had been hours now. The last I saw of them, they were outside apparently arguing, but certainly it was too frigid to remain there for too long. I wondered if they were still outside, so I casually walked over to the large glass windows and peered out. No one was there. I glanced at my watch, stunned at how late it had actually become. Eleven-thirty. Wow, I had been talking to his family a long time. What a tiring day—driving in from Albuquerque and getting settled into the rental, then shopping, and now this event. I was ready to leave.

I turned and ventured across the room, seeing a hallway I hadn't been down. Maybe they were in Peter's office or something. If not there, I'd nose my way up that grand staircase. Worming my way through the partiers, I noticed Greg's family had already got in on the dancing action. Gene and Betsy were doing their best seventies moves right along with Tammi. They all sure seemed tight knit, which I still found odd, but nice that neighbors remained friendly for so many years.

Someone grabbed my arm from behind as I passed by the dancers; I whirled around. It was Dana.

"Hey, where ya hiding my brother?" She was gasping

for air, and still wriggling her body with the music. "Haven't seen him in hours."

Raising my voice above the noise, "I know! I'm looking for him myself. Any ideas? He was with Peter."

She stopped dancing, took my arm, and we swiftly moved to the side. I told her I was going to hunt him down, and she wanted to go with me.

"I wanna see more of this fantastic home. I can't believe how well Tammi made out—look at all this!" Dana's jaw gaped, looking around.

We turned down a long hallway. There were open doors all along the way. Several bedrooms—empty. One room was a 10-seat movie theater. We stepped in, heard some groaning, and saw a couple making out. It was not Greg or Peter, thank goodness, so we continued down the hallway, leaving the lovebirds alone.

At the end of the hall was a staircase descending below the main level.

"I hadn't realized this place had a basement," Dana mentioned.

We descended the stairs and discovered another long hallway. I figured we must be under the great room that was upstairs. We peered into each room. Again, so many guest rooms ... I'd counted at least eight so far. All were empty. At the end of the hallway, there was a living area not that much smaller than the upstairs version, but it led outside through giant doors. We looked through the windows and didn't see signs of anyone having been out there. Fresh snow drifts were at least a foot high piled along the exterior, there was no footprint evidence of traffic through this exit.

"This whole downstairs area could be a complete apartment for an enormous family. Look over there, another full kitchen!" Dana exclaimed. She walked into the kitchen, admiring it, and running her fingertips over the cool marble countertops. "I'd love a kitchen like this." I nodded. Exhausted, my patience was running thin at this point. I wanted to go to bed.

"Look, Libby!" Dana had opened another door into an enormous wine cellar.

A light was on, so we entered, calling Peter's name. No one answered. Wine racks stood in front of us, as far as we could see. Each aisle labeled with the red, white, or sparkling varieties stored there. "Jeez, how much money does this guy have? This is insane."

I agreed with her as politely as possible, trying to keep my sarcasm to myself. Yes, I think everyone here is sufficiently impressed by Peter Schull's accomplishments. However, I was ready to leave, and my only goal now was to find Greg. I debated between being worried about my missing boyfriend, or having someone drive me home and worry about him in the morning. I mean, he was amongst family and friends—would it be rude of me to leave without him?

"Let's head back upstairs. Maybe they've resurfaced now."

Dana was chatty all the way back upstairs. Despite my grumpiness as the evening wore on, I found her to be a gracious lady. As we ascended to the main level, she never skipped a beat. She extended an invitation for us to visit her family in Pagosa Springs; she mentioned they'd love to come to Arizona (only not in the summer—she couldn't handle the heat), and she topped it all off by telling me about a recent vacation they took to New Orleans and how miserable she'd been with the heat and humidity. As we neared the living area, I noticed one of the previously opened bedroom doors was closed now. I quietly knocked, while opening it, and stepped in, turning on the light. Nope, it was vacant as well.

One more search of the party floor and I was determined to leave. As soon as we rounded the kitchen corner, into the expansive dining area, there he was. He turned and gave me one of his classic gorgeous smiles. It faded when he saw my expression.

"I've been looking all over for you," I said quietly, moving in on his right side for a small hug. "I've been worried."

"Oh, sweetie," he leaned over and kissed the top of my head. "Let me introduce you to my other friends."

The two men standing with him gave me a nod.

"Libby, this is Michael Thorn and Neeraj Prasad—my roommates from college that I told you about. Guys, finally you get to meet the one I've talked about all night!"

Neeraj stepped closer. "Please, call me Raj. It's a pleasure to meet you, Libby." His eyes were kind and held mine for several seconds. With prayer hands together, he bowed his head slightly. I immediately took a liking to Raj.

"Hi Libby, I'm Michael." His eyes shifted between Greg and me, then cast out over the crowd distractedly.

"The guys have been showing me around. It's unbelievable the company they created since we left college. I'm stunned." Greg explained, taking a sip from a water bottle.

Speaking of being stunned. I had expected a long explanation for where he's been all evening and that was it? For all I knew, he or Peter killed each other outside.

I turned to address him quietly, without the friends,

"Listen, hon. I'm exhausted. It's been a long day, and sounds like tomorrow will be even more fun-filled," I half-heartedly laughed. "Is there a driver that could take me home?"

Apparently, I wasn't quiet enough because Michael pounced on my question. "Right out the front doors. You'll see a line of SUVs, with our drivers. They are prepared to take guests home whenever you're ready."

"Thank you, Michael," I nodded, then turned to Greg. "I'm going to head back. You have fun."

He looked worried. "Wait. Are you sure?"

"Enjoy your friends and *family*," I made a point of saying. "We'll catch up over breakfast in the morning."

He leaned over and pulled me in for a long kiss. "Thanks, Lib. It's been a long time since I've seen my friends. I appreciate it!" He took my hand and led me out the front door.

Michael was right. There before us was a long line of black-tinted SUVs—a Secret Service-like procession. With this display, you'd have thought this party included the President of the United States, maybe foreign dignitaries. Greg assisted me into the back seat of the lead SUV and shut the door, blowing me a kiss. As we pulled away, I glanced back. Standing in the mansion's doorway was Tammi, her smug expression the last thing I saw as we rounded the corner.

CHAPTER SIX

I felt Greg crawl into bed around two-thirty. At least he was safe and sound, I thought as I fell back into a deep slumber until around nine o'clock. When I awoke, his side of the bed was empty.

I stretched out, debating whether I actually wanted to get up. The smell of bacon infiltrated my senses, which was encouraging. But instead of moving, I found my eyes closing again, my mind a slideshow recounting conversations from the night before.

In my thirty-eight years, I've never considered myself a jealous person. My family and friends have described me as a confident, successful, and independent woman. That's who I am. Maybe a little stubborn, but certainly not insecure or jealous of others. So, *why have I awakened now, feeling insecure about last night?*

I heard footfalls nearby, and I softly peeked through my lashes. Greg stood over me smiling, then sat at the edge of the bed and took my hand.

"I'm sorry for the late nights, hon." His eyes held mine. He lifted my hand and kissed it tenderly. "I didn't expect this. Honestly. But I'm enjoying seeing everyone again. It'll be over soon."

"Don't worry. It's nice you're having fun with your college buddies," I sat up, giving a slight chuckle. "I've even had a little fun seeing you completely hungover for the first time." I hesitated, choosing my words carefully, and deciding to be forthright about my feelings. "What bothered me last night was being blindsided."

His head hung, and he squeezed my hand tighter.

I cautiously explained what it felt like to learn his family knew nothing about me. And, Tammi—that was a surprise.

"Hey, I did not know that Peter even knew Tammi. I haven't seen her since my sophomore year in college, Libby. Trust me, I was as blindsided by that as you—and Peter—were. And my parents being here—I didn't see that coming either. Guess everyone wanted to surprise me." He rolled his eyes. Then mocked, "Yay, surprise!"

"Why hadn't you mentioned dating me? To your parents..."

He sighed. "Libby, remember when you didn't want your mother to know about me?"

I nodded.

"Well, similarly, my family can be overbearing. And, it's true, Mom has always adored Tammi. There's nothing I can do about that. She's pestered me about her since high school." Flustered, he stood and paced the room. "Dad stays out of it, thank goodness. Dana has been hot and cold about Tammi, but for some reason, they all stayed in contact with her." He stopped and glanced over at me. "By the way, I didn't know that part until Dana told me last night."

"Oh, I learned a whole lot from your family over dinner," I stated.

He continued pacing. "It shocked me Peter even knew the same Tammi. And I think you'd agree that I was genuinely surprised by that, right?"

I nodded.

"Since she and I broke up *twenty years ago*, I always thought Larry would go after her. *That* wouldn't have surprised me. But, Peter? No. Never saw that coming. He never knew I had a previous relationship with her."

"You left the party pretty upset with Peter. What happened?"

"Oh. We went outside, and he told me all about meeting her … at a charity event in Albuquerque. They hit it off; the rest was history." He shrugged and sat back down on the bed. "My initial reaction was that there was some type of conspiracy. How could this woman worm her way into my decades-long friendship? I thought I was done with her and now I learn she's marrying my best friend from college. Pete helped me to understand that there was nothing nefarious going on—except maybe coincidence. By the way, when I was dating her back in high school, her last name was Miller. Peter had only mentioned her by first name during our phone conversations. And the wedding invitation included her current last name, Hansen. There's no way I could have known they were the same person."

"So, she's been married before," I surmised.

"Several times, from what I understand. In fact, that's

what led Peter and me around the property while he showed me his collection of cars, artwork, wine cellar, and more. I questioned whether he was certain this was the woman to marry; you know, with her multiple failed attempts. Also, I expressed concern about whether they were rushing into things. Was there a prenuptial agreement, for example? I found myself more worried about that bit as he continued to showboat his wealth." He stood again, clearly concerned about his friend. "Libby, I think he's in over his head. Only maybe that's my bias against Tammi?"

I looked questioningly.

"When she latches on, she doesn't let go. It took me a long time to get rid of her. That's why I wasn't pleased to learn my mom has kept up contact all these years."

Everything made so much more sense now. Tension releasing from my shoulders, I reached out for Greg's hand on his next pass by the bed. "Hey, it's okay. I understand."

"Sorry for leaving you all evening. I came looking for you a couple times, but man, was that place crowded?"

I nodded, remembering the partiers whooping it up.

"Then Michael and Raj showed up and, of course, Peter wanted to give them the tour. I wanted to catch up with them as well, so I went along."

"It's okay. I understand." That's when something popped into my head. "Night before last, you mentioned a Hector. He drove you home from Peter's in Albuquerque. Was he there last night?"

"You know, I never saw him. Doesn't mean he wasn't there in the crowd, though."

"Did he go to college with you?"

"No, they hired him later. Think he mentioned MIT? Anyway, I met him for the first time during the bachelor party night."

We both heard Joshua running down the stairs, followed by more footfalls which turned out to be Shadow. They both barreled through the doorway, Shadow jumping onto the bed and smothering me with kisses.

"No … off the bed, big black dog!" I struggled a bit, but got her off.

"Mom says breakfast is ready!" Joshua yelled, then turned about-face, and tore off down the hallway again. Shadow chased.

"Guess we better get up there…" I said, removing the covers.

* * *

Alexis went all out. Omelets, bacon, fresh fruit salad, and a couple of carafes of coffee already brewed. She must have known we were out late, even though we each tried hard not to wake them in the middle of the night.

Once we finished eating, Greg headed for a shower. JJ wanted to check out the equipment in the garage, so he headed outdoors. Joshua and Shadow ran back to the game room, leaving Alexis and me stretched out on the sectional sofa in front of a nice blazing fireplace. The morning was particularly cold. According to the forecast, they expected a polar plunge which would dip the local temperatures into the minus territory. More snow was imminent in the coming days, which I actually looked forward to. Nothing wrong with sitting by the fire and relaxing while on vacation.

"Sounds like it was quite the party," Alexis commented, taking a sip from her coffee mug. She caught my eye-roll. "What? Did you not enjoy yourself?"

"Oh, I did. There were several surprises that Greg

failed to mention when he related last night's events to you guys over breakfast."

"Oh, yeah. What happened?"

I updated her on the revelations. Her eyes widened, riveted to my tale.

"He had no idea?" she muttered.

"Which part—parents' attendance or former cheerleader girlfriend? Oh, yeah … doesn't matter; he didn't know about either."

"Don't you find that unbelievable?"

"Initially, yes. We talked this morning, though. I mean, of course I believe him—I don't think he's trying to be deceptive. The unsettling part for me is this Tammi. My instincts say *she* is cunning. The fact that she's secretly been in touch with Greg's mother for all these years …" I shook my head and took another sip of coffee. "Then she invites them to the wedding, knowing Greg is the best man; I don't know, but something smells fishy here. To me, it seems she manipulated the secrecy. But why? Maybe I understood that incorrectly, I don't know. He was shocked, though. You should have seen his face. I literally thought he ran to the bathroom to hurl."

Lexi's hand flew up to cover her mouth. "You're kidding me. He just ran from the room?" she laughed. "Well, poor guy, he wasn't actually feeling well yesterday after his late-night drinking. It surprised me you both lasted as late as you did last night."

"Yeah, I'm sorry about that. I hope we didn't wake you. I tried to be quiet."

"So, you *did* come home at separate times. I thought I heard two different vehicles pull up. Why weren't you together?"

"That was the other not-so-fun part about last night.

Greg disappeared early on and left me to get to know his family on my own."

Another look from Lexi.

"I know."

Eventually changing the subject, Lexi asked what today's plans were and mentioned they were headed to the ski area shortly. They got Joshua into a ski school around one that afternoon.

"Oh, shoot. That reminded me—the wedding party, they're skiing, starting at eight this morning. Guess we missed that. How do they party all night and then make plans for eight?"

"Who skis on their wedding day? I mean, is this normal behavior for you white folks? I know it's not in my husband's family, but jeez," Alexis laughingly questioned.

I assured her it wasn't cultural, but maybe another pretentious trait of the rich and famous—who knows. However, we settled on being grateful for the use of the fabulous accommodations they'd provided.

* * *

Once showered, I found Shadow at Joshua's feet, playing games in the playroom. I coaxed her away from her little buddy and bundled up in our warmest clothing to set out for a walk. I was thankful for the fenced yard, so I didn't have to walk her every single time she needed out. But she also needed actual exercise and I could use the fresh air as well.

Greg joined us and we set out down the main road. The homes were sparse on this street, which also meant little traffic. Once I got used to my boots on the snowy roadway, we managed a decent brisk walk.

"I guess we missed the ski plans this morning," Greg mentioned.

"Yeah. Alexis said it best. Who goes skiing on their wedding day?" I laughed.

"I guess those two do!"

We chuckled about all the over-the-top stuff and he told me more about last evening. When we approached the house on our return, we trudged through the snow at the side of the house.

"I want to see how this would work—skiing from the house. I imagine we have to get our passes at the ski lodge first, though."

"Oh, no, there are passes for each one of us sitting on the kitchen counter."

"For the Johnsons too? They've thought of everything, haven't they?"

I nodded.

We rounded the house and entered through a side gate. I removed Shadow's leash once we were secure in the fenced yard. It wasn't a huge space, but plenty of room for her to explore, sniffing out all the squirrels and wildlife. We walked through a separate gate that led to the ski hill, leaving Shadow in the yard.

"I'm not sure I like this," I said, pointing to the ground.

Greg, still with eyes ahead and on the ski slope, added, "What's not to love? You can literally ski out from here. Means we don't have to drive and fight for parking space."

"No, hon, stop. Look."

He was a couple of steps ahead of me and then turned around. His eyes finally looked where I was pointing at on the ground.

"Aren't those our footprints from yesterday when we got here?"

"I don't think so. We stopped back there several feet." I walked back a few steps and pointed out our indentations in the snow versus the new ones.

"Hmmm," he scratched his head. He slowly examined the ground and then walked methodically following the prints northwest which led to the Johnson's wing of the home. They ended right in front of their patio. We looked up, Alexis was pulling back the curtains, and we startled her. She waved and opened the French door.

"What are you guys doing out there?" she shivered.

"Did either you or JJ walk out to the ski run from your patio yesterday?"

"No."

"Makes sense, Greg. Look. The prints are only going this direction—toward the house. They aren't shown with the toe-end headed back to the forest, or ski hill. Where do they go?"

He examined closer. Then, continued carefully walking over the patio and toward the far side of the house. He called back to us, "Over here. They pick up again—appear to go around the house."

I went back and grabbed Shadow, who started barking her discontent about being left alone. Alexis went inside to put on warmer clothing and said she'd join us out front.

As we rounded the house, JJ came out from the garage, staring curiously.

"Come here, man," Greg shouted. Once JJ made it to us, Greg pointed to the snow. "Someone walked from the ski hill, up to your wing's back patio, and then around the front of the house here."

JJ slowly shook his head. "Well, I don't like that." Our experienced detective friend went into investigative mode. He backtracked, pointing out that there were actually two sets of prints, other than the ones we'd obviously created. One track was a sizeable boot print, the other much smaller. "I'd say a man and woman, judging from the sizes. This smaller one could even be a child's, actually."

Greg kneeled down in the snow. "Hey, look. Isn't this a brand logo or something?"

JJ examined closer. "I think you're right. Got your phone with you?"

I pulled mine from my pocket and quickly handed it to JJ. He snapped several photographs, then we went back inside the warm house.

Alexis greeted us at the door. "Did you see where the tracks led?"

Greg nodded. "JJ thinks as we do—they're fresh. You didn't hear anything last night, did you?" He removed his jacket and boots, leaving them in the foyer. We followed suit, and I hung up Shadow's leash on the same hook with my coat, and we set boots underneath the long bench.

Neither Alexis nor JJ had heard or seen anyone last night. "All was quiet. Maybe it was in the afternoon when we were bustling around getting settled?"

Greg thought about it. "I don't remember seeing anything when we walked the several feet beyond that gate yesterday."

"Or maybe it was while we were in town." I threw the possibility out there. "I don't think we went out back again once we returned and before we left for the evening. Maybe it was a parent and child who got turned around trying to get back to their vacation rental?"

Despite JJ's healthy dose of detective skepticism, we all chalked it up to lost vacationers; it was the most logical explanation.

"Well, the Johnsons are going skiing shortly. What's our plan for the day?" I asked Greg.

He picked up the wedding weekend packet from the kitchen counter. As he read, he lifted his wrist and checked the time. "Looks like there's a brunch that's started already for those who weren't skiing … about half hour ago. Not hungry, but I guess we could make an appearance for that, couldn't we?"

I nodded. We finished getting ready and put Shadow in her crate since the Johnsons were also heading out. While locking up, I glanced out our back windows toward the ski hills. An unsettled feeling washed over me.

CHAPTER SEVEN

The entire wedding day passed quickly with a well-planned, nonstop agenda. Neither the bride nor groom had attended the morning brunch after skiing. The rest of the guests enjoyed the lovely spread, however. Apparently, once the bride and groom came off the hills, the wedding party was busy getting pampered somewhere; I'd imagined it as an ordeal to get all spiffed-up for the big moment. How did women handle all that? Honestly, I'd rather elope than be part of such an enormous production. To me, it seemed to be a waste of money, time, and effort. Wouldn't the money be better spent on a really nice honeymoon, a new home, or *anything else*? Of course, I was certain this couple never had that concern; they clearly enjoyed all that an exquisite wedding entails, and I could also imagine that included some fancy honeymoon.

By the time the nighttime wedding came around, I finally met Hector Salazar. He was the one business associate I hadn't met the night before. He was friendly, down-to-earth, and so unlike the others. I hadn't picked up on any pretentious vibes from him as I had with Michael; Hector was serious, and I could tell his hands were full as lead scientist and innovator at the company.

I also met Peter's parents. Anne and Bill Schull were clearly proud of their son's success. That's all they raved about. Anne was pleasant; Bill, quite full of himself.

What I found most remarkable was the absence of Tammi's family. At least I hadn't been introduced to anyone, and no one mentioned them. This morning at the brunch, I had assumed her mother must be assisting with the beauty regimen, but would her father go along for all that? Seemed unlikely. And where were all of Tammi's friends? I'd only met friends of the groom; none from the bride's side. To listen to Betsy and Anne talk, Tammi had been the popular cheerleader back in the day. Where was her posse now? Well, there was the one screeching microphone gal from the night before, I guess.

It was late evening by the time the nuptials would begin, and we were back in the couple's home. They had moved all their living room furniture out. In its place, white foldable chairs were set up in precise rows. A gorgeous altar platform showcased the warmth of the fireplace at the head of the room. They'd adorned the enormous space with beautiful flower bouquets in various shades of white, beige, and maroon, everywhere. The guests' white chairs had shimmering beige chiffon chair sashes expertly placed with similar sprigs of flowers. Soft lighting, with glowing candles, shimmered on every surface. Similar chiffon, intertwined with tiny lights, cascaded the length of the grand staircase.

A nice young gentleman ushered me to a seat; now, I was eager to see who the bridesmaids were and what they were wearing. That's when I noticed they sat me in the same row as Greg's parents, only a couple of rows from the altar. Neither Dana nor Larry was with them, and I soon learned why.

The classical music began and everyone turned toward the entryway's grand staircase. Greg and Tammi's friend, the microphone gal, were the first in the procession, arm in arm. He found me in the audience and smiled. My heart swelled; he was handsome in his black tuxedo. Next came … *Dana?* That surprised me—she hadn't mentioned being one of Tammi's bridesmaids. She and Peter's business partner, Michael, smiled toward the audience as they navigated the stairs and made their way into the room. The gentlemen joined Peter on the right-hand side and the ladies on the left. Each bridesmaid wore a gorgeous burgundy velvet gown with a sweetheart neckline, three-quarter sleeves, perfectly fitted through the bodice with a wide black satin ribbon tied as a bow at her mid-section, and then finished with a tailored, elegant A-line skirt. I hadn't seen bridesmaid's dresses as nice as these. One more pair began down the steps—Larry and a girl I hadn't seen previously. Again, I found it interesting that no one in Greg's family previously mentioned their participation in the wedding.

The *Wedding March* music sounded, and we all stood in anticipation of the bride's entrance. Raj accompanied her down the stairs to her groom. She was every bit the beautiful bride, fulfilling that fairy tale role, as though Disney scripted the entire production. Her gown was a similar style to the bridesmaids', only fancier. She was gorgeous in her pink champagne-colored dress, complete with the same black satin belt effect. A delicate veil draped over her face and an impossibly long, lacey train trailed behind her down the aisle. She took everyone's breath away. I looked over at Peter; his smile stretched from ear to ear.

It wasn't long before the nuptials concluded. Everyone congratulated the newlyweds; standing in line to greet the entire wedding party, including the parents. While we waited our turn, I finally asked Betsy about the absence of Tammi's parents.

"Her parents were killed in a tragic car accident when they were children. They were raised by an aunt," she explained.

"Ohhh," I whispered, feeling that familiar pang of knowing what it was like to lose a parent at a young age. She lost *both*. Guilt spread through me considering my judgement of the woman so far. "And where's her aunt now?"

She shrugged. "I'm not sure I've ever met her, actually."

Another pang. "No siblings, I take it?"

"Oh, you haven't met Abby yet? You'll meet her here in a few minutes."

I finally met the dancing, energetic, microphone girl—she was Tammi's sister, Abby. I had seen the resemblance last night, only I assumed it was the typical styling that most close friends choose these days. That Kardashian look-alike hair and makeup that many young women copied now. Abby had Tammi's exact shade of platinum blonde—her petite, thin frame was identical. Seeing them side by side, I could tell that Abby's face was slightly fuller, not as sharp as Tammi's. Both wore thick, expertly applied makeup, like Hollywood stars.

I stood on tiptoes and whispered in Greg's ear, "Did you know Dana was going to be Tammi's maid of honor? That was surprising; your sister hadn't mentioned it last night."

"Yeah, had no idea. They were friends back in the day, but I don't think they've kept in touch for years now. I'd have thought Abby would have stood with her."

After going through the receiving line, they encouraged everyone to find their coats and make their way to the large wooden decking outside the rear of the home. For fifteen minutes, we stood watching in awe as fireworks lit up the night sky. Greg leaned down, lifted my chin slightly, and gently kissed me.

"I'm so happy you are in my life. Thank you for joining me for this," he breathed.

"Nowhere else I'd rather be," I smiled up at him. "Well, actually, it's warmer inside. I don't think this attire is meant to be worn outside in the winter."

He chuckled, and as soon as the last firework went off, we hightailed it back inside and straight to the fireplace.

This night we danced and celebrated love. Everyone drank too much, and the antics got wilder as the night disappeared into early morning.

* * *

Mid-morning, we finally awoke; Greg reached for his phone, which had pinged. His friends were raring to go again.

"Ugh. Wow. They're all gathering for another group ski. *How?*" he groaned, stretching as he sat on the bedside.

I rubbed my eyes. How could it be time to get up? "Doesn't mean you have to go…" I suggested.

"Yeah." His yawn bellowed. "Last day of events. I should make an appearance. *We*, if you're willing—but no pressure." He got up and closed the door to the ensuite bathroom.

I stretched out, still considering. Despite my initial exhaustion, I really wanted to go skiing, and the doctor had cleared me to go. I'd probably have energy after a couple mugs of coffee. Lifting my wrist above me, I made circles with it as if to prove it was ready for the slopes. By the time Greg exited the bathroom, I'd already put on my first layer of warm clothing.

"Sure, I'll go skiing with you guys this morning. And then maybe see if Lexi wants to head to town later for girls' shopping and stuff."

He pulled me into his arms. "You make me so happy. What a wonderful weekend this has been, Ms. Madsen. Now, let's grab some coffee. I'll text the group to let them know we'll meet up soon."

* * *

The twinsies, as I was now referring to Tammi and Abby, could be seen from miles away in their hot-pink ski outfits. Nearly neon ski pants, black jackets showing off the same pink color as adornments, complete with rhinestones which caught the sunlight. Each wore cream-colored furry beanies with their long, blonde ponytails protruding. Their gloves also matched their jackets, sparkles and all. As we came to the bottom of the hill where they were standing, the surrounding snow glowed pink.

Michael, Raj, Peter, and Greg could have all been twins themselves. Each had on all black, except Raj stood out with this blue knit cap and blue goggles. The rest of them favored their aviators to protect their eyes from the blinding sun. Michael preferred snowboarding over skiing.

"Perfect morning!" Tammi exclaimed. "Better get our slope time in now. Storm is coming this afternoon, I hear."

With that, I tucked my auburn hair into my red beanie, and pulled my gloves on. Greg and I followed the group over to the largest lift—the gondola. Riding to the top of the mountain, I marveled at the scenery; snow-covered slopes as far as one could see. I pointed out to Greg what I thought was our rental house in the distance, off the slope we'd ventured down from the property moments prior. There was a smaller ski lift closer to it; I banked that to memory.

It'd been a couple of years since I'd been skiing. Once we were at the top, Tammi and Abby shot off in one direction, headed to a black diamond run. Peter and the guys turned to us.

"Over here are some blue runs—not as difficult— what sounds good to you?" Peter asked Greg.

Angst plastered on my face. Greg grinned and then turned back to them. "I think we're good at trying some green for now, since this is our first outing this weekend. We'll catch up to you, though. How's that sound?"

Relief appeared to wash over Michael. Peter nodded and the two of them took off after Tammi and Abby down the black run. Raj considered for a moment and decided he'd hang out with us. Hector ended up trailing behind Michael and Peter several minutes after they'd left, apologizing to us, and mentioning he'd ski with us later.

Following Raj, we stabbed the snow with our poles to get started, moving like skaters to gain momentum. We settled into a comfortable rhythm; Raj taking the lead, then me, and Greg brought up the rear. Despite the glaring snow in the full sunshine, the air was frigid against my cheeks. It wasn't long, and I felt my legs balancing on the skis well—muscle memory taking over; like riding a bike, they say. Knees bending, hips leaning into each turn, it was exhilarating as the skis scraped the snow-packed hill with each move. Legs stretching upright, then bending, angling for the snow again … and again. All my focus right in front of me, traversing the slope, savoring the sights, smells, and sounds.

I could no longer see Raj ahead of us; he was that fast. I wasn't going to concern myself with speed; he could beat us to the bottom of the run. I glanced back at Greg briefly, catching his radiant smile; he was still following close, but not too close.

I was out of breath when we caught up to Raj at the point where two runs intersected. We stepped off to the side, checked our map, and went for the blue— intermediate—option. Off again, gaining momentum as we approached the steeper slope. This one would get us back to the front of the mountain, where we could pick a new ski lift.

Several snowboarders sped by, stirring the frigid air and startling me. I watched them violently slashing the snow as they crossed their way down the hill. They went immediately out of sight. My heart settled, and I regained my rhythm again.

By the time we made it back to the ski lodge, I was ready for a break. We slowly skidded to a stop at the bottom of the slope, used our poles to punch down on the binding's release, and stepped out of the skis. I heard the horrific scraping sound before registering what was happening. Another snowboarder, wildly out of control, had slammed into a poor woman standing with her family. Expletives flew from the woman's mouth.

Greg rushed over to offer assistance. Before he got to her, the snowboarder had bailed; he hadn't even stopped long enough to ensure the lady was okay. I locked Greg's and my skis to the closest rack and then joined him where the crowd had gathered. The lady was back on her feet, insisting she was fine, even though she kept wincing with her hand on her right hip. We encouraged her to go inside and ask for ski patrol help.

"Oh, I'm okay. Just going to grab some lunch and rest a little in the lodge. I'll be fine. Really."

Several bystanders stepped up to offer their phone numbers, including Greg. "Listen, just in case … we can help identify the guy. You never know what injuries you've got once the adrenaline wears off. It probably would be a good idea to get checked out by a doctor."

She politely took the information and smiled. "Thank you. There are still decent human beings in the world. I appreciate your help." Her family helped her into the lodge. I watched her hobble for the first few steps, as she slowly navigated the steps into the building.

"Sure hope she'll be alright. That was an awfully hard hit," Greg muttered. "I can't believe those snowboarders. Up on the hill, that one guy could have taken you out, too."

I nodded in agreement, then changed subjects. "Ready

for lunch? Maybe some hot chocolate?" I shivered, pulling my gloves back on. The brisk wind coming from the north cut through my layered clothing. "Maybe that's where Raj ran off to?"

Apparently, everyone had the same idea. We stood in a long line, waiting to order cheeseburgers and hot chocolate. While we waited, I scanned the room, looking for Raj, but never found him or anyone else from our party. The injured lady and her family were sitting in a far corner near the windows.

"After lunch, wanna head back up the mountain? Or have you had enough for today?" Greg asked, pulling out the map from his jacket.

"Maybe let's take this lift." I pointed. "This takes us to this blue run. Which will ultimately lead us back to our house." I smiled at him.

"Sounds like a plan. If we don't run into the gang prior to that, I'll head back with you. Would you mind if I continued skiing if we find them, though?"

"Of course not."

We ordered and then waited for our number to be called. The aroma from the green-chile cheeseburgers was amazing. We dove right in and savored every bite. I was far hungrier than I'd thought. That's also when I realized how tired my muscles were; definitely a great workout, but ready to be done for today. We gathered our jackets, gloves, hats, and sunglasses. I glimpsed the lodge doors as the wind slammed them shut; the pink reflective glow on one of the twinsies as they walked in was unmistakable.

"There they are," I stated. "Looks like you'll have friends to ski with after all."

"I can see you back to the house and then meet up with them."

"Oh, don't be silly. I can find my way back. Go have fun!"

We caught up with Abby, Peter, and Hector; they were waiting for the others to catch up, they said. Greg confirmed they were still planning to ski after getting something to eat and asked about joining them.

"Of course, man. Both of you?" Hector was thrilled.

"Nah, I'm tired—will head back," I mentioned.

Greg excused himself, letting them know he'd be right back.

With a gentle hand on my back, we walked up the steps and found my skis amongst hundreds locked up on the racks. I geared up, stepped into my bindings, and leaned into him for a delicate kiss.

"You sure? It'd be nothing for me to ski with you home and then get back here … probably even before they make it through the food line."

I shook my head. "No, really. This will be nice—a little solo run. Good reflective time." I smiled broadly, turned, and maneuvered over to the ski lift.

He stood there and waved to me as I sat down on the chair and floated up the hill.

CHAPTER EIGHT

High above the ski hill, scanning the snow-covered forest, and seeing the small skiing figures below, I thought of little Joshua. I'd forgotten to ask how his ski lessons went. I looked forward to skiing with my friends for the rest of the week. All the more reason to not wear myself out on the first day. I stretched my wrist again, feeling a twinge of soreness, but no pain from my previously injured arm. I looked ahead; we were about halfway up the hill.

In the far distance, clouds were building. The chilly breeze continued. I noticed myself crossing my arms in front of my chest, huddling to keep the heat in. I glanced down at one run when a pink reflection caught my eye. Had to be Tammi—her outfit was unmistakable, and we'd only seen Abby in the lodge moments prior. She was talking to someone, stopped at the side of the slope nearest the tree line. Hopefully, neither had fallen. Lifting my arm, I started to wave and call out to them before quickly aborting that plan.

Certainly, I had seen that all wrong, I thought. Looking ahead, this ride was ending, and the ski lift operators were approaching rapidly. I held both poles in my right hand and scooted to the edge of the chair, preparing for the exit. Once I'd managed myself over to the side, and out of other skiers' way, I strained to see down the hill where Greg's friends had been.

From high above the ski run, I'd swore Tammi had leaned in to the person she was talking to. It appeared quite intimate—*had they been about to kiss?* Certainly not. My mind raced; there had to be an explanation. Peter, her husband of less than twenty-four hours, I knew for sure, was in the ski lodge below. So, maybe it wasn't Tammi? Reason told me that wasn't true, either. I'd talked to Abby in the lodge, for one. Second, those custom-made hot-pink ski outfits stood out and the only other person who wore one today was Tammi. I couldn't help myself; I pushed off and headed down the run toward them.

Not far along, I could see the distinctive pink off in the distance. The two figures were quite close together—hugging, maybe. I slowed, taking my time and steadily swooshing my way to see closer. I angled in their direction, positioned to pivot and turn away again, and I could definitely identify the pink-suit wearer as Tammi. The super blonde, very tiny physique, and sparkling diamond on her ungloved left hand were unmistakable. The other person had their back to me, unfortunately. Dressed in all black, and not even a tuft of hair emerging from the red knit cap, I couldn't see who she was with. *Weren't all the male friends wearing black today—was this one of Peter's friends?* Of course, there were many skiers dressed in all black—could be someone else entirely. Then I remembered how they'd had black beanies on, so that ruled out Peter's immediate friends. Most importantly, it ruled out Peter. I quickly made my next turn, trying to get another glimpse slightly farther down the slope. Nope, I couldn't tell who she was with, but I felt certain it was someone she knew well.

There was only one direction I could go now, so I skied to the bottom of the run. Hurriedly, I made my way directly to the lift line, which thankfully was short, and I got right on. Slowly lifting uphill again, my impatience was building. I had questionable vibes from Tammi from the moment I met her, but this was unthinkable. *Poor Peter!* A flash from the rhinestones on her suit, and my head twisted around to see them skiing away. Dangit. I missed my opportunity. *Would I really have confronted them, though?* Probably not.

Once I exited the lift this time, I took the fork in the run that positioned me toward the home where we were staying. I easily found it, trying to keep my downhill momentum to make it most of the way on the cut-out trail before I had to use my poles again. At the gate, I released my bindings and stepped out from my skis. Shadow was on the other side of the windows, barking madly until Alexis opened the door. My pup came barreling toward me as I locked the gate behind me; I kneeled to welcome the puppy love.

* * *

After a nice long soaking bubble bath, I checked my

phone. Greg texted that they were still having fun. He'd be back by suppertime. The regional storm due to arrive within the next twelve hours wasn't forecast to hit this area until midnight. My vote was to hit town today because tomorrow's drive might not be possible. That gave the Johnsons and me plenty of time to explore Taos before Greg came off the slopes later in the afternoon.

We pulled into the historic Taos Plaza and parked. Despite the weather forecast, at the moment the sky was blue, the sun glared, but it was definitely chilly. Bundled in layers, we walked around the historic district. Immediately, I saw the bakery Sage had mentioned—Sweet's Sweets.

"Before we leave, I'd really like to grab something from that bakery," I pleaded, pointing out the cute shop with purple accents. "It comes highly recommended."

JJ nodded. Alexis' eyes widened excitedly. Shadow gave a low woof, and Joshua hopped up and down. All in agreement, we agreed to hit that on the way out of town. We set off across the parking lot and then strolled along the sidewalk, gazing into shop windows. Alexis and JJ were particularly interested in the art galleries. I couldn't take Shadow inside, and Joshua already looked bored, so we went our separate ways for a little while. They shopped the galleries; we walked, and window shopped. Joshua and Shadow had become inseparable little buddies.

Crossing North Plaza, we walked around a farmer's market for a while longer. I picked up some fresh produce, and then we casually made our way back to the rendezvous point—Sweet's Sweets bakery. Alexis was already inside talking to a lady when I realized I probably shouldn't bring

Shadow inside. I motioned to her through the window, pointed at Shadow, and sent Joshua in.

The lady Alexis was talking to—I estimated her to be in her mid-to-late fifties, with short salt and pepper graying hair—smiled widely. She radiated kindness and immediately came to the door. She came outside, knelt down, and cooed at Shadow, "Who is this sweet one?"

"This is Shadow," I explained. JJ walked up then, and without words, took Shadow's leash from me and motioned for me to go inside.

The bakery owner stood again. "Hi! I'm Samantha Sweet. Please, come on in."

"Thanks!" I said, following her in. "I'm Libby Madsen." I looked back and saw JJ and Shadow settling in on an outdoor bench. Shadow appeared unsettled, intent on seeing in the door where I disappeared.

Samantha leaned down again, this time her attention focused on the young boy who'd snuck in behind her and hung tight to his mother's legs. Joshua's deep brown eyes slowly peeked out from around Alexis. "Now, you must be Joshua. Your mother was telling me about you. Hey, I know just the thing for you. Of course, only if mom approves?" she stood, looking at his mom. My friend nodded.

Sam grabbed a frosted cookie from the display, put it on a napkin, and handed it to the little boy.

"Thank you!" his excited little voice squeaked, emerging from behind mom and snatching up the cookie.

Samantha laughed heartily. "Works like a charm every time. Hey, Alexis was telling me a friend of yours from Arizona recommended my bakery and that's what brought you all in today."

"Yes! Sage Logan told me we *had* to stop here and say

hi. She raved about your bakery," I explained.

"Oh, wow. *Sage*. How is she doing?" Sam instantly remembered the artist. "I mean, it's been so long, and I know it was rough after Tom passed."

"She's doing great. Yes, it's taken her several years, but she's resumed painting and sculpting. She has an excellent network of friends and stays plenty busy."

A customer walked in, and Sam excused herself while she helped the lady.

We took the coffee that Alexis had already purchased and took seats at a nearby bistro table. "I figured I'd wait for you before purchasing baked goods. Sam highly recommended their house brew," my friend smiled, doctoring hers with fresh cream. Joshua was still busy chomping away at his decorated snowman sugar cookie. His mouth and cheeks glistened in silver and light-blue glitter.

I leaned over and stared at the enclosed glass bakery case from our table. It was filled with goodies. Donuts in several varieties, beautifully decorated cupcakes, scones, and holiday decorated cookies. There were cakes, pies, holiday slices, and tartlets as well. I admired the three-tiered cake on the front window display. It was a gorgeous winter scene, complete with skiers traversing the slopes and snow flocked pine trees. It was stunning.

On the table, I picked up a flyer advertising a gingerbread house decorating contest. All ages were welcome. I handed it to Alexis.

"This looks fun …"

"He'd *love* it," she tilted her head toward the cookie monster. "So would I. Should we sign up?"

I read the flyer again, this time paying more attention

to the details. I noticed it was scheduled to begin in about an hour. We were probably too late to sign up.

"You guys want to stay around longer?" I asked my friend.

Sam walked up with a small plate that had bakery samplings. "Ah, saw our flyer, I see. How long will you be in town? Maybe you'd like to join us for this?" she asked, setting the plate of bite-sized goodies down and giving me a wink. "Thought you ladies might want to sample before making a purchasing decision?"

"It's not too late to join the contest?" Lexi asked.

"Not at all. We had two groups cancel last minute, unsure if the weather would cooperate late afternoon. We'd love for you to join—we have plenty of room!"

I looked outside at JJ and Shadow. "Um, maybe this afternoon isn't the best time?" I mentioned.

Samantha immediately added, "They can join! The contest begins right after I close shop." She looked outside at Shadow laying at JJ's feet. "She'll be fine, don't worry."

Alexis popped outside and discussed it with JJ. Moments later, she came back, nodding her head.

Joshua yelled out, "Yay! Gingerbread man!"

I grabbed a bite-sized piece of the turtle brownie and popped it in my mouth. Rolling my eyes in ecstasy, "You must have known that any friend of Sage is a connoisseur of chocolate!" I wiped the corners of my mouth. "These are *fantastic*, Sam."

"Thank you!" she said, getting distracted by another customer walking in. "Ladies, I'll be right back. Little short-handed today," she grinned.

Alexis took a bite of the apple-spiced cheesecake cookie. We sipped coffee; neither of us talked much as we thoroughly enjoyed the small bites. I glanced out the front windows and saw that JJ and Shadow were no longer waiting for us. They'd gone for a walk.

"JJ doesn't mind waiting for us?" I asked Lexi.

"No, he's going to join the contest," she smiled.

"Of course, he is. What was I thinking?" I laughed. JJ was always up for anything—such a sweet man.

Business never slowed down for Samantha. After we'd finished our snacks and coffee, we got in line and ordered several items. Joshua was most interested in the decorated cookies. Alexis eyed the small version of a caramel-pumpkin cheesecake. For me, brownies; always. I mentioned that should last us the week; Alexis looked at me like they *might* last the evening. We confirmed the timing for the gingerbread house decorating and promised we'd return.

* * *

An hour later, they led us into the backroom where we joined several ladies, who were already standing at the long worktable. Samantha, along with her trusted employee, Becky, had all the cut-out pieces for several gingerbread houses spread out on parchment paper.

Two ladies immediately fawned over Shadow. However, I caught the look from another lady who stood ramrod still and hadn't yet cracked a smile; she seemed familiar, but I couldn't place exactly where I'd seen her before. I began feeling insecure about having brought Shadow inside.

Sam handled it like a pro. "Libby, Alexis, your group can be at this end. Shadow should fit in nicely at your feet, I'd think." Her smile instantly relaxing me.

JJ and Alexis slipped in on either side of me, with Joshua at his mom's side. Everyone around the table introduced themselves. We all paired off into teams as we were seated around the table: JJ and I, Alexis and Joshua, Sarah and Nancy, and finally, June and Naomi. Then, we carefully listened to instructions from Becky. She set out several bowls of frosting in a variety of colors and explained how the judging would work. The winning team had to finish within the two-hours allotted time. They would judge based on the most creative, colorful, and spectacular looking gingerbread house. The winner got a specialty cake of their choice and their creation displayed in the bakery's front window. The team who finished as runner-up received a free large box of baked goods from the bakery case.

We all expressed our excitement when the prizes were revealed. Sarah, the lady who seemed out of place, cracked a thin smile. Even though earlier I felt her glaring at me, I thought she might loosen up a little by now. She was intense—was this going to be a cutthroat competition? *Or had she taken exception with me, or Shadow?* I wasn't sure, and I couldn't imagine *why*.

With gingerbread pieces in front of each team, Becky gave an 'on your marks' countdown and we were off, constructing houses. We all chit-chatted as we frosted the walls together into a standing three-dimensional structure. June and Naomi were clearly pros at this—all four of their walls were standing, while JJ and I were still trying to get two of ours to stick together. I heard Joshua *tsk* at his mother when one of their side walls fell. I chuckled to myself. Upon waking earlier, completely exhausted, I hadn't dreamed I would have skied several slopes, walked around the Taos Plaza, *and* joined a bakery decorating contest, all in the same day. What fun it'd turned out to be!

A quietness had settled within the room. Each team's sheer concentration was evident as they mounted the roofs on their structures. JJ and I were holding our breath, praying ours wouldn't collapse; I was sure the others felt the same. Samantha and Becky sat off to the side; friendly observers, probably happy to be off their feet for the first time all day. Hearing a dramatic groan, I lifted my eyes to see Nancy as the recipient of Sarah's classic nasty glare. I wondered what Nancy had possibly done wrong, but focused my eyes back on our own project. I also considered whether Sarah was friends with any of the other ladies. *What was her story?* She exuded tension—*was she that serious about this contest, or maybe unhappy overall?*

JJ nudged me, and gave me a look that I read as, 'get back to work'. Once all the structures appeared to be held together, the conversation eventually resumed. We learned Naomi wanted to bring her granddaughters, but they wound up with colds and couldn't join. She looked at Joshua.

"How old are you, young man?"

He shyly smiled at her. In a tiny soft voice, he answered, "Five."

"Oh yes," she nodded. "My two little granddaughters are four and six. Too bad they couldn't come."

I caught Sarah rolling eyes like that would have been disastrous to have *three* children here. June and Nancy began their own stories of their grandchildren, and that's how the rest of the afternoon went. I shared stories of my nieces and nephews. Joshua even opened up and shared favorite family holiday traditions with the ladies. Eventually, we got around to everyone in the room. And they all had advice for us tourists about what to do in Taos before we left town. Samantha wanted us to stop in at the library and say hi to Emily, her family's librarian friend. June and Naomi raved about coming back during the summer and touring the old pueblo outside of town. Nancy spoke about a half dozen restaurants we *had to try*. Sarah didn't offer anything. She only furiously worked at decorating the gingerbread house. I wondered if I was the only one who saw her casting angry looks about.

Becky gave the 'fifteen minutes to go' call and everyone gasped. Where had the time gone? JJ and I hurried to give last-minute touches to our classic design. He put into place the last of the colorful gumdrops along the roofline. I finished 'gluing' on equally brilliant, round chocolate candies all over the walls. There were bushes of sugary confections decorating the front garden, with rock candy trees, and a stone walkway also made from candy.

Joshua and Alexis picked out Marvel comic colors and hoarded the candies to match. In the end, theirs was a superhero gingerbread house. June and Naomi went for the English garden look. Sarah and Nancy made a wintry, snow-covered house with dramatic icicles and frozen features. When the buzzer rang, and all our hands went up to show we were done, that was the only smile I had seen from Sarah. She was clearly proud of her creation. Nancy was not.

"Okay, feel free to take a break and stretch your legs. Head to the front of the bakery to refill coffee and Sam has set out some snacks. We'll begin the judging process and call you back when we're ready."

I grabbed Shadow's leash, and we followed the group

through the door to the front. JJ suggested he'd like some fresh air, so he offered to take Shadow with him, which I appreciated; it was getting dark out already.

Joshua ran right up to the snack tray and grabbed a colorful cookie.

"After all the sugar he's had today, this car ride home should be fun," Lexi whispered to me.

I chuckled and pulled my phone from my pocket. There were several messages from Greg.

Are you back from Taos yet? 3:30 p.m.

Still at the ski lodge—waiting for Peter. 3:31 p.m.

No Peter. Lifts have already shut down. Still waiting. 4:30 p.m.

Libs, where are you? 4:45 p.m.

Still no Peter. Concerned now. 5:02 p.m.

"Oh, jeez!" I said aloud, achieving a groan from Sarah and a gasp from Lexi.

"What?" my friend leaned in to ask.

"Greg and his friends are still at the ski lodge. I expected them to have left hours ago." I lifted my wrist to check the time. "Last message only a few minutes ago."

Her large brown eyes sought mine. Hesitantly, she whispered, "Everyone okay?"

"They can't find Peter. I'm going to step out and call him back," I mumbled, walking out of the front door and pushing the call button.

"Libs! Where ya been?" Greg sounded concerned.

"We're still in Taos. Decided to join a fun …"

"Listen, Libby … Peter is missing."

"Missing? Like, officially *missing*?" My pulse quickened. "What happened?"

"Tammi is frantic. My family … his family. *Everyone* has

skied every slope looking for him. No one has seen him since lunchtime."

"What? Maybe he went back to their house without telling anyone?"

"Several people are there—no sign of him."

"Oh." I was speechless. "Where would he have gone?"

"That's what we're trying to learn. Most of the morning he was skiing with Raj and Michael … the girls for a while, too. But after lunchtime, no one has seen him."

"Oh, jeez. I'm sorry, hon." I twisted around when I saw the bakery shop's door open. Nancy peeked her head out and motioned to come back in. The results were about to be announced.

"Hey, Greg. We're about to leave here shortly. Should we meet you at the lodge? Or, the rental?"

"I'll meet you at our place. See you in thirty. Oh, and hey … be cautious, storm is moving in." I looked up at the darkened cloudy ski. Several flakes had fallen, but I hadn't considered it *stormy* yet. Still, I agreed we'd be careful, regardless.

I hung up; JJ and Shadow rounded the corner. We headed back inside, where we found everyone patiently waiting by the gingerbread house displays. Becky stepped forward with her clipboard and made the announcement.

"After much deliberation and appreciation for each work of art, the runner-up prize goes to …" she paused for dramatic effect, smiling widely. "June and Naomi!"

Everyone clapped and congratulated June and Naomi.

"And, the grand prize winner of a specialty cake and featured display of their gingerbread house goes to …" she paused even longer this time around. "Alexis and Joshua!"

A loud bang sounded. Sarah had slammed her palms

against the countertop. She huffed and stormed out of the room, mumbling something under her breath. We all jumped when the door slammed behind her. Then we heard the tinkling bells as she stormed out the front door. Samantha looked horrified. Becky stared wide-eyed, confused about what to do next.

Joshua yelled, "Yay!!! Mom, we won!" He danced excitedly.

His sweet, youthful voice broke the awkward silence and reminded everyone to congratulate the winners. Samantha helped Joshua move his gingerbread house to the front window.

Alexis smiled proudly at her son. She leaned closer to me and whispered, "What a spoilsport that lady was, huh?"

I scanned my friend's expression. Thank goodness she hadn't heard what the crabby lady said on the way out. "Sheesh!" I shook my head in disgust.

The other ladies hugged Joshua and Alexis, then bundled up and said goodbye to everyone. I saw outside the front door that the snow was really coming down now.

"Samantha, thank you so much for all this. You and Becky really made our afternoon."

Sam pulled me aside and whispered, "Listen, I'm so sorry …"

I cut her off. "None of that was your fault. Please…"

"I heard the racist comment she said about your friends. From their reactions, I believe they missed it—thankfully. But, still … I'm mortified for *her*."

Both of us casually looked through the doorway at the Johnsons.

"Is Sarah someone who frequents here often?"

"Oh no, no. Just met her today. In fact, immediately

after you all left earlier, she came in. Saw our flyer in the window and wanted to join. I've never seen her around here before."

I remembered Greg's call and felt anxious to leave.

"Again, Sam, it was so great to meet you. If we're back in town later in the week, we may come in again and grab up some treats for the road trip home. If not, I'll say hi to Sage. And, if you're ever in Arizona—please look up Dharma Inspired Day Spa. We'd love to treat you!"

"Definitely. If in Arizona, I'll most certainly reach out." She held the door open. We walked back to the front counter, where the others were still chatting away.

She turned to Alexis. "Oh wait! Almost forgot, you guys get to order a custom creation. Wanna place that order now?"

Joshua was jumping up and down excitedly. Alexis turned to me, knowing that I was eager to get back.

"Samantha, we're here all week. Could we think about that for a little bit? We'll call and come back…"

Sam was already reaching for one of her business cards from the counter. "Here's my number. And, I hope to see you all real soon," she patted Joshua on the head again. "Congratulations again, young man. You had a super creative idea."

His eyes widened with pride.

"Yes, I saw that was all *your* idea. Your mom followed your lead. Good job!" she smiled and held the door open for us as I ushered the group outside.

"Again, nice meeting you, Sam," I said.

CHAPTER NINE

The cloud ceiling had fallen low, swallowing the canyon ahead of us. I turned on the fog lights and concentrated hard on the winding mountain road ahead of me. Although I couldn't see a vehicle ahead, I carefully followed the established set of tracks and moved along slowly.

"This moved in fast, didn't it?" JJ said.

"Snow!" Joshua screeched from his car seat in the back, startling me.

Shadow gave out a low woof in answer to her buddy.

"I haven't driven in snow in so long," I mumbled, focusing intently on my only job now. "Sure is getting deeper the higher up the mountain we go."

Quietness enveloped us as we cautiously moved along.

Slowly, and meticulously, we crept our way to our rental home, only spinning the tires in our own driveway where the snow had accumulated at least a foot.

I let Shadow out of the back and she bounded through the white fluffy frozen substance. Her smile was wide, yipping at the falling flakes. Joshua chased her once his mom set him down on the ground. Shadow and the young child ran around, rolling in the thick white blanketed yard; we stood laughing at them. JJ picked up a handful of snow, rolling it into a ball, throwing directly at his son. He nailed him on the back and then it was a full-on snowball fight. That's when I looked back at the path we'd been on. Our driveway had no tracks before we'd pulled in. Where was Greg?

I grabbed the keys from my purse and left the Johnson family to play. Opening the front door, I yelled out, "Greg!" as I removed my winter garb, leaving it in the foyer.

I ran to our wing of the home. "Greg, are you here?"

No one answered. I ran back to my purse and removed my phone, frantically finding his name in my call log and pushing the button.

"Sorry, hon. Should have called sooner," was how he answered. "We're at Peter's house now."

"Did you find him, then?"

"No. Unfortunately. And now that the weather has moved in, it's getting serious. Ski Patrol, Sheriff's office, and a local search and rescue team organizer are here now talking to the family. Libby, I'm worried."

"Well, of course you are. What can I do?"

"Right now, stay put. This storm is only going to get more intense as the night goes on. The sheriff has been adamant—no more vehicles on the already treacherous roads. Ice will be the next concern as the temperatures plummet."

Thinking of the drive we'd completed, I was grateful we'd left town when we did. The sheriff was right.

"So, you'll stay at Peter's tonight, then?" A twinge of uncertainty crept along my spine. What was I concerned about—Peter's disappearance? Tammi? Greg's safety if he tried to drive home? Definitely, it was the distraught bride seeking solace from my boyfriend.

"Yep. Gonna have to."

"Okay. Hey, what leads do they have so far?"

He explained the entire afternoon's events. After I'd left, he visited a few minutes with Peter, Abby, and Raj. Peter didn't stay around for lunch. Apparently he was eager to get back on the slopes. Greg hung with Abby and Raj, waiting for the rest of the group.

No one else came in for lunch, so he joined Abby and Raj; they went to the top of the mountain. He skied with them for about an hour, but they were so much more advanced and he was tiring out. Greg headed back to the front of the mountain, skiing on some easier runs, and eventually settled back at the lodge with a beer, waiting for everyone.

Abby was the first to join him; she grabbed a peppermint Schnapps hot chocolate. It wasn't long before Hector came in and called it a day; he went back to his place. Tammi texted her sister and said she had to pop into town before the night's events. Greg continued to wait for Michael, Peter, and Raj.

Close to the time that the ski lifts were due to close, Raj came down the last run with several ladies in tow. They were laughing and carrying on as they bounded into the lodge. Many other skiers had already cleared out. Food was no longer being served, but the bar was still open. Greg assumed people were keeping their eyes on the storm and probably wanted to get safely back to the cabins before it hit.

Apparently, Raj had been skiing with the ladies most of the afternoon. He didn't know why Greg thought he'd been with Peter, but was concerned that no one had seen them since lunchtime. Since the ski lifts had already shut down, Raj went over to the ski patrol building and let them know—Peter and Michael were still on the mountain somewhere. They put out a call on their radios to alert all patrol stations across the ski resort. About that time, Michael finally answered Hector's texts. He had left the ski hills an hour ago and was already back at his cabin. He hadn't seen Peter since before lunchtime, either.

"We waited. It got dark. Despite the encroaching storm, the ski patrol had checked all ski runs and gave the 'all clear'. No sign of Peter. That's when they called the sheriff. We'd already confirmed with Peter's family that he hadn't shown up yet at their house."

"Wow," was all I could get out as I stared out into our backyard, watching the heavy snowfall. That's when I remembered. Only, I didn't know exactly how to bring up what I had to tell him. "Um, Greg. I saw something earlier. Completely forgot about it until right now."

"Yeah, what is it?"

"Well, ummm. You know when I left you earlier and took the lift to ski back to our place?"

"Yeah."

"Uh, I saw Tammi," I hesitated. *Had I seen everything clearly?* I certainly didn't want to spread gossip. "Yeah, I saw

Tammi—you know, her bright pink outfit and all."

I sensed his impatience. "Spit it out, Libs. What did you see?"

"From the ski lift, I thought I might not be seeing things accurately. So I skied down the hill..."

"*What* did you see, Libby?"

"Greg, Tammi with someone. Looked fairly intimate to me. And it wasn't Peter. Remember, I'd just left you with Peter moments before that at the lodge?"

The silence was palpable.

"You still there?" I asked.

"Yep. That wit..." he stopped himself. "She's up to it again!"

"Up to what?"

"Libby, I've gotta go. You all stay inside and stay warm. Once I confirm the roads have been plowed, I will come home."

"Okay. But, what about Tam..." He'd already hung up.

An unsettled feeling crept over me.

CHAPTER TEN

We woke to at least three feet of snow. I immediately called Greg for an update. There was no update, but the snowfall had blocked all roads throughout the resort area. He wouldn't be home soon, not until the plows went through.

With a heavy heart, Shadow and I made our way to the kitchen. Through the windows, I could see the Johnsons had cleared a path into the backyard. Joshua was already out there, frolicking in the white powder. Shadow barked, and I let her outside to join him. They were in heaven.

After a cup of coffee, we adults joined them, playing in the snow, making snow angels, and building snowmen in the backyard. By late morning, and after some hot oatmeal and cocoa, we heard the plows go by on the main road.

Greg called shortly thereafter.

"Sheriff says the plows should have the resort area cleared by early afternoon." His voice sounded heavy, tired.

"Did you get any sleep last night?" I asked.

"A little—fits and spurts, but we're all happy to see clear skies this morning. That means the helicopters can now survey the area."

"Still haven't heard anything from him?"

"No. Calls are all going straight to voice mail."

"Have they been able to track his phone?"

"They're working on it, but haven't heard anything new this morning."

"How's Tammi?"

"Oh, she's a hot mess. Distraught and mostly hidden away in their master suite since she got in late last night. I think she's only allowed Abby and my mom in there."

I was grateful that Betsy was there for Tammi in her time of need. My heart sank, thinking about how I'd feel if it were Greg missing. I wanted to know, "With the roads almost cleared, what's the plan?"

"Well, they assembled the search and rescue teams already, and the sheriff's department has set up a command center at the ski resort. Peter's home has become the location where friends, family, and volunteers have gathered. As it stands, those of us here when the storm arrived make up that team, but I heard Raj on the phone bringing in reinforcements. Apparently, they know everyone in the region."

"What can we do?"

"As soon as Peter's driveway is clear, I'll come home. In the meantime, I'll try to get more information and determine where we could be most useful."

"Has anyone checked the cellar?"

"What?"

"That enormous climate-controlled wine cellar with the bomb-shelter-like door…"

He laughed. "Oh, yes, of course. The family has combed this entire home. We weren't able to do anything outdoors last night, however. Maybe that's where we could help. Shadow sniffing around the property couldn't hurt, right?"

"Yes! What if Peter attempted to ski back home, suffered an injury, and hunkered down somewhere?"

"Doesn't explain why he didn't call or answer his phone."

"Could have fallen and lost it, though…" I added.

"That's true. Anyway, I should be able to make it home within maybe an hour or so. Can't wait to get out of here, honestly. I've felt a bit trapped, you know?"

"Couldn't even imagine. See you soon!" I hung up, eager to see him.

* * *

Shortly after one, we pulled up in the parking lot of the ski lodge. I unloaded Shadow from the backseat and held tight to her leash as we made our way to the building that said Sheriff on it. The area was buzzing with activity— skiers and ski patrol personnel scurrying about, and we dodged our way among the crowd and into the building to find someone in charge.

I looked around the room and discovered some friends and family members had gathered here as well.

"Greg! Where is he?" Tammi sobbed, launching herself into Greg's arms.

Caught by surprise, he awkwardly patted her back. "Tam, I don't know. Has there been anything new since I left the house earlier?"

The crying got worse. She was wracked with sobs and couldn't answer. She only shook her head and shrugged her shoulders. I looked sympathetically toward both of them, but couldn't help but think the display was a little over the top. Eventually, she released her grasp and moved on to Michael, who had just walked in.

"Oh, Michael!" Once she clutched onto him, we skirted away.

Greg glanced around, looking over people's heads. "Over there. That's the deputy I was talking to earlier."

We walked over to him and he set down his coffee.

"Ah, you must be the wife Greg was so desperate to get home to last night? I swear—he was going to crawl through that storm to get home to you, if I hadn't physically detained him," he bellowed.

Greg laughed. "Derrick, this is my girlfriend, Libby Madsen. And this is her puppy, Shadow. And Libby, Derrick exaggerated the whole detainment bit!"

"Oh, my bad. I assumed y'all were married the way you gushed and all." He bent down and petted Shadow on the head.

"Very nice to meet you, Ms. Madsen. Beautiful Lab you got there."

I nodded and shook his hand. "We'd like to help find Greg's friend. Maybe Shadow…"

"Ah, we got a canine team, if needed. But thank you anyway." His smile was friendly, his tone showed his authority.

"Sure. But, please … anything we can do to help, we'd love to."

Another deputy walked up then, and we took our cue to stay out of their way. So that's what we did. Greg ventured over to Tammi and Michael. Shadow and I meandered around the room. I caught bits and pieces of conversations: *he always pops off on little adventures; well, you know, their stocks plummeted once the FDA started investigating— I'd run and hide too; I heard he fell off a cliff; the biggest surprise is that* she *didn't leave* him *at the altar; he probably ran off with a cute little ski bunny.*

It really was too much, people already gossiping. I saw Dana from across the room and went over to her.

"Hey, Dana …"

"Oh! What an adorable dog!" she exclaimed, reaching out and making friends with Shadow. "We used to have a Lab—his name was Chuck. Named after our grandfather, Charles," she giggled.

"So, were you stuck all night at Tammi's place, too?" I asked.

"Oh yeah, that storm was a doozy, wasn't it? I still can't believe Peter never came home. Kept expecting him to walk in at any minute."

"Was your family on the slopes yesterday—had you seen Peter all day?"

"No. Mom and Dad exhausted themselves on the wedding day. They hung out at the cabin most of the day. I took the boys sledding—there's a nice place for it down the way," she pointed. "I'm not sure what Larry did. Haven't seen him since … hmm, well, since the receiving line at the wedding, maybe? Oh no, there was a woman he was dancing with that night … wouldn't surprise me if that's where he went, you know…" she gave a teasing wink.

"But you all were at the Schull household last night, right?"

"Well, the parents and me with the kids. Yes. They had a super nice taco bar set up, late afternoon. And, the margaritas were flowing, let me tell you! Whew! It was good the roads weren't clear to leave—none of us had any business driving anywhere."

And I had pictured an evening where all the guests were wringing their hands and crying over Peter's disappearance. Sounds like that wasn't the case at all. I asked more questions; by then, Betsy and Gene joined our conversation. No one could remember the last time they saw the groom. Since none of them had gone skiing yesterday, their comments were mainly reminiscing about the wedding night. I stood around listening to their stories. *Was there something from earlier in the weekend that might explain where he disappeared to?*

The more I thought about the wedding night, I realized that I'd spent more time with Greg's family than with anyone else from the wedding party. Tammi and Abby had been the life of the party. Both danced incessantly with *everyone*. I couldn't recall Peter dancing, but certainly he had been. Right?

Betsy and Gene were concerned, but not overly. I turned to my right, sensing someone approaching. It was Peter's parents.

I reached out and gave each of them a hug.

Peter's mother, Anne, had worry etched on her face. However, once we got talking to both of them, it became evident they weren't exactly all that worried, unlike the bride and others in the room.

Bill was pragmatic. Stoic in his stature, he simply stated, "I don't know what all the fuss is about. I'm sure he's out skiing or snowboarding. The kid doesn't ever sit still long, you know." He blew on his hot coffee, then took a sip.

Anne rolled her eyes. "Bill, why then wouldn't he have come home last night? I don't know, I can't make sense of him sometimes. Why wouldn't he tell Tammi where he was going? I mean, they *are* newlyweds—you'd think they'd want to 'sleep in a little' this morning," she used air quotes and grinned in my direction. "I can see why she's upset. Poor girl, left alone now so soon after her wedding." Her fingers found the Danish she'd been holding in a napkin; she picked another piece off and popped it in her mouth.

Surprised by their indifference about their son, I stayed quiet.

Gene became resolute. "Bill, I tend to agree with you. What has Michael, Raj, or Hector said?"

"Oh, I haven't talked to them. Maybe Tammi has?" Bill answered.

I leaned into Dana, whispering, "Peter's parents were at the house with all of you last night?"

"No, they were snowed in at their home."

I assumed they had been staying in the enormous Schull household all along. So, the Lawson's were there, but not Peter's parents. No wonder Betsy consoled Tammi. Looking at Anne now, however, I'd have guessed she wouldn't have been much comfort in the situation. I sensed that tight-upper-lip mentality with his parents.

Gracefully bowing out of the conversation, I led Shadow away from that group and found Greg still with Tammi.

"Hey, Tammi," I gently approached.

I thought she was going to cry again. I gave her a hug. The three of us found seating. After several minutes, I dove right in.

"Tammi, would you mind sharing with me what happened yesterday?"

"Ugh. That's all I've been talking about," she welled up again.

"Sure, I understand. When you're ready. It might trigger something that could ultimately help the authorities, though."

She nodded, wiped her eyes with a tissue, and after several seconds, she relived her entire wedding weekend. Greg went off in search of coffee; he'd heard it all. I didn't attempt to stop her chattering, even though I was itching to learn who she'd been with on the slope. For now, it was important to listen, though. Who knew which detail would wind up being the most important? I listened intently to her for the next forty-five minutes. During that time, the room filled with more family and friends; the noise level soared in the lodge. By the time she wrapped it up, Michael had walked up to us. She stood, and he took her into his arms. I overheard him telling her not to worry. He seemed to believe the most logical scenario was that Peter went off on one of his typical adventures and he'd walk through those doors shortly.

I ducked away and found Greg with his parents now. They were trying to lure everyone back to the Schull home so that the rescue teams and authorities could effectively do their jobs back at the resort. Slowly, but surely, the crowd dissipated, and we followed along behind the procession of black SUVs.

When we walked into Peter's home, delicious aromas hit our noses. Another spread of food? I supposed all of it was the pre-planned part of the wedding weekend; obviously, they'd already paid for it and the caterers kept showing up on time. Certainly, the family was not considering *partying* after their son went missing, right?

As we ate, I listened to various theories from the family. One thing was obvious; no one except for the bride was truly distraught. I mean, Greg and friends were concerned, but the overwhelming reaction was that this appeared to be normal behavior from the groom. He frequently took off on adventures and had done so his whole life. So, who called the authorities if his own family wasn't concerned? I wasn't sure, but it had to have been Tammi.

Before we lost daylight again, I wanted to take Shadow around the home. And we might as well snoop outside. I left Greg with his parents, telling him I was taking Shadow out.

First, we searched the home; I guided her through each room ... upstairs, downstairs, and through all wings. While in the primary suite, I snuck a man's t-shirt from the laundry hamper and had Shadow smell it. We continued snooping around; Shadow was sure excited to be scouting, but she never alerted to finding anything of concern. I'm not sure what I expected really, Shadow had no formal rescue training.

We headed outdoors to the back of the house. Similar to our rental, there was a pathway that led to a ski slope. We followed the path to the edge of the run, looking through trees, and then up and down the slope.

SWOOSH!

A snowboard flew past, covering Shadow and me with a spray of snow and startling us. *Darn snowboarders!* We turned back toward the house.

Shadow pulled me into a copse of trees to our left. She excitedly smelled her way, and I dodged snow-covered limbs, cringing every time snow fell down the back of my neck. I'd grabbed my heavy coat before we left the house, but I hadn't remembered my knit hat or gloves, and I was only wearing jeans, which meant we wouldn't be out here for long. The sun was low, and the temperatures were dropping quickly. I began wondering if what his family said was true. If so, I sure hoped Peter had gone off on an adventure—somewhere inside, where it was warm. Only that wouldn't explain why he hadn't called anyone yet. I couldn't imagine him being exposed outdoors for this long. And, I was sure that's exactly what the authorities were concerned about and why they were taking this far more seriously than the family.

By the time we approached the house again, the snow was belly deep on Shadow, which meant I was up to my knees in it. She leaped over mounds of snow with a huge smile plastered on her face. Whatever had gotten her attention as we made our way into another grouping of trees, she was laser-focused. Around one tree, over a snow-covered downed log, and then through deeper snow. I followed obediently until I realized we'd made a complete circle and were now chasing our tails.

"Come on, Shadow," I sighed. "Is there something here ... or is it only a squirrel?"

She kept plowing forward, happily pulling me in tow. After not seeing one trace of human footprints, I stopped her.

"Let's go this way!" I cheered her on, changing direction toward the house.

We stopped in the mud room before entering the house. I slipped off my wet boots and found a towel to wipe off Shadow's paws.

"What a klutz," I declared when I dropped my phone. Kneeling down in front of the mud room's bench, I peered underneath and reached cautiously, feeling around for my device. "Got it." I pulled out a phone, only it wasn't mine. This one had a heavy-duty black case; mine was colorful, with hand-painted mandalas. The screen saver image popped on with a selfie of Peter and Tammi on a boat somewhere. *Was this Peter's phone?* I gently set it on the bench, found a scarf hanging on a hook nearby, and grabbed it.

Quickly, I kneeled again on the floor, reaching under the bench, and I finally found my phone. I shoved it into my pocket. Walking into the living room, I saw Greg by the fireplace, talking to Raj.

"Where's Tammi?" I held up the phone I'd found now encased in a scarf. "I think this is Peter's."

"Where'd you find it?" he asked, taking it from me.

"Careful! What if it becomes evidence?" I pointed out, gathering up the scarf that fell.

Vigilantly, he wrapped the scarf around the end of the phone. "I think she went back to her room," he finally answered my initial question, his voice solemn. "Libby, Peter goes nowhere without his phone. Where did you find it?"

CHAPTER ELEVEN

It was the final night of the wedding weekend. I wanted to look forward to us spending time with our friends, skiing, exploring, cooking, and enjoying our vacation. Instead, we felt obligated to help with the search.

"Think the family is taking it more seriously now?" I asked Greg.

He tipped the bottle a little more, pouring the rest of it. Looking back at me, he handed me my glass of pinot noir. We both took a sip, looking across the room at Anne and Bill huddled with the Lawsons.

"Hard to say. I think so."

"Not very emotional people, are they?"

He shook his head. Then, both of us turned toward the front door when it abruptly opened. Shadow barked, running out of the room. That, and a flurry of activity, got everyone's attention. I ran after Shadow, grabbed her harness, and pulled her back to the mudroom that sat off the entranceway. Grabbing her leash from a hook, I snapped it on before leading her back to the living room. Several cops had entered, walking straight over to Peter's parents. I couldn't hear what was said, but I saw that one officer handed something over to Bill.

Anne's hand swiftly covered her mouth; her eyes were full of worry. We saw Betsy put an arm around her as we walked over to them.

Greg approached Peter's dad. "What'd they find?"

"Sunglasses."

"And, they're Peter's?"

He nodded solemnly.

I noticed what he was holding. They looked like the same aviator-style glasses all the guys wore. "How can you be sure they are Peter's?"

He turned them on their side, pointing to the frame's left arm. "See here. His logo."

"Ohhh." I wondered if he was the only one who wore the company's logo. I'd ask around.

The police told us they found them near the ski racks outside of the lodge. They informed us that after reviewing camera footage from all the ski lifts, their focus was now within the ski village itself. Their teams had combed the slopes earlier; it was their belief that he was no longer on the mountain. Of course, if he had gone off the trail, that was a different story. A helicopter had done several passes and would continue again in the morning, weather permitting.

Greg let an officer know that we'd found a phone

suspected to be Peter's. He explained his wife had it now. He guided the police to where they could find Tammi and the phone.

Once the officers left the house, a sadness washed over the household. It was real. It seemed Peter was actually missing.

Anne sought her husband. "I need a car—please get me out of here," her eyes looked frantic. More emotion than she'd displayed all day, I thought. Bill took her by the arm and they left.

Greg's parents stood speechless.

Dana asked, "How's Tammi?"

"Upset. Concerned. Really, she only wanted to be left alone." The warmth of the wine coursed through my body. I removed the sweater I had on and wrapped it around my waist. Then I looked at Dana again. Something had been nagging in the back of my mind. "I know you've known Tammi since childhood. Must have always been close—I mean, being her maid of honor and all?"

Flustered, she took a second. Then she smiled and answered, "Well, I'll be honest … we haven't always been that close. In fact, there were several years we lost contact altogether." She glanced around the room, presumably making sure no one was overhearing. "Libby, I honestly have no idea why she chose me as maid of honor. It was the strangest thing. However, none of my closest friends ever had the big weddings. I'd always wanted to be maid of honor. So, I accepted without even really questioning anything. Why?"

"Oh, must have been something Greg said … I got the impression that you and Tammi weren't close."

"Well, he's right … but also, I've really tried to befriend

her recently. You know, it was an honor when she asked me." She shook her head, momentarily looking confused. Then, she chuckled, "I'll say, though. She's a difficult one to get close to. Super guarded."

I wondered what Tammi's full story was. So far, I'd learned that she was a cheerleader in high school, had a few failed marriages, stayed in contact with Greg's family to a degree, and now married his best friend who was missing. There was more to this story—I was sure of it.

Greg walked up and Dana said she'd go find another bottle of pinot to top us off.

"Have the police questioned Tammi yet?"

He looked suspiciously at me. "I assume so. Why?"

"Wouldn't she know him best?"

He nodded. "The whole family still mainly believes that he had wandered off, although they're concerned now that his phone and sunglasses have been found."

"Then why the police presence?"

"Mainly because of the huge storm last night. Temperatures dipping in the sub-zero range. The ski resort definitely has motivation to be sure they left no one on the hills after dark. They don't want to be sued."

I nodded, considering that. Made sense.

"What do you believe? Is your friend 'being Peter'?"

"I don't know, Libby. Sure, back in the day—in college—he was dismissive and only consumed by having a good time. He'd run off with other friends, mostly *women friends*, and he'd not be seen for days. So, I know what they're saying. However, I also think he's been a responsible adult for many years now as well."

"Any mention from his partners about the health of the company?"

Now, I got the whole squinted face reaction. "What? Where are you going with this Libby?"

I waved a dismissive hand. "It's probably nothing. Just gossip."

"No. What have you heard?"

"When we were at the lodge earlier, and Shadow and I were walking through the room, I overheard many theories amongst the group."

"Like what?"

"Many surprised the wedding even took place … you know, the old dogma about being left at the altar. Both sides—meaning, some surprised she showed up; others stunned he went through with it."

"Really?" He glanced around the room again. "What does that have to do with the health of the company?"

"One mention was related to the FDA … um, if I remember right, 'the news is about to break wide open' … something along those lines. Know anything about that?"

"No!"

"Maybe one of the guys would be able to confirm or deny?" I suggested.

He stood, shaking his head, considering. "I can try…"

Dana swept in and filled each of our glasses from a fresh bottle of wine. She set it down on a table next to us. "Just in case," she winked.

"Dana," Greg approached. "Know anything about Peter's company?"

"Nothing. I don't even know what he does…"

"But Tammi hasn't mentioned any related troubles, has she?"

She shook her head, her eyes moving between the two of us.

"What about their relationship? Was she getting cold feet?" I asked her.

"What is this? The Spanish inquisition? Since when are you two detectives?" she laughed heartily, snorting, which got all of us going. I admired the humor in Greg's sister more and more.

Many of the solemn guests heard us laughing and stared in our direction. I guess it was inappropriate at this time.

"No, seriously," she spoke in hushed tones, "Tammi adored Peter. She never spoke ill of him at all. If anything, I think she wished they had more time together. He worked an awful lot. But I know for a fact, she enjoyed the finer things in life … so what could she expect? I mean, he's got to work for all this!"

I nodded. Betsy and Gene were on their way over to us, so I put on a smile. When asked, we shrugged off the earlier laughter as a childhood memory the siblings shared.

Betsy appeared distraught. Obviously, she considered Greg's friend part of the family.

"Poor Anne," she said, sounding pensive. "I don't know how they're holding it together."

Greg put his arm around his mother. "Seems to me they still think Peter is off having a good time somewhere."

She looked up at him, horrified. "Greg!"

"I'm just saying, Mom." He gave her a kiss on the head, then stepped back, looking her softly in the eyes. "We'll find him soon, I'm sure."

"It's getting dark out. Should we head back to our place? Maybe your family would like to join us and meet the Johnsons. Hey, where's your brother anyway?" I noticed he hadn't joined the family all day.

Simultaneously, Gene shrugged and Betsy asked, "Who are the Johnsons?" And rolling her eyes at my question, Dana said, "Larry's probably picked up some hottie last night. The guy never stops."

I laughed at Dana, while Greg explained the Johnsons were our friends, my longtime besties, and Alexis was my business partner. They agreed to follow us to our place.

CHAPTER TWELVE

Monday morning and we still had an entire week of vacation ahead of us. Something about the excitement of it all had diminished, though. Greg and JJ sat at the breakfast bar, sipping their coffee and talking about Peter's disappearance. Joshua and Shadow's footfalls sounded like elephants running from one end of the house to the other, so I bundled them up and sent them outside. Alexis was enjoying a luxurious bubble bath in her suite, while I stood near the fireplace, watching my godson and pup through the window, romping in the snow.

I overheard the guys' conversation.

"It seems suspect that a newlywed would just take off … without explanation. All his family and friends are around," JJ pointed out.

"I know. That's what doesn't sit well with me, too."

"I'm still enjoying the part where you learned he was marrying an ex-girlfriend of yours," JJ chuckled. "That's gotta be awkward!"

Greg wasn't as amused. "*High school!*" he emphasized. "Ages ago. But, yeah, I didn't know that before this weekend. It was extremely strange they'd hooked up many years later. Small world, I guess, huh?"

I turned around, walking away from the window.

"What was Tammi like back then?" I asked.

Greg's eyes glanced upward, thinking, "What do you mean?"

"Does she seem the same person as she was back then? Or has she changed a lot since then?"

"Hmmm. Hard to say. In the short time we've been here, I'd say she seems about the same. She's always been that girl who dressed well, had her hair and makeup just so, and worried how others saw her. Seems that hasn't changed."

JJ added, "Sounds pretentious to me."

Greg grinned. "It's one thing I couldn't stand back then. Now, don't get me wrong—I'm also sure it's what attracted me to her in the first place. But, honestly, she was a *lot* … always concerned over her looks, status, being part of the 'who's who.' It was exhausting."

I giggled to myself. That's precisely how I saw Tammi, which is what struck me so oddly that she and Greg had ever dated. My initial impression was that they were polar opposites. That reminded me about what I had seen from the lift and how he'd been upset when I told him.

Greg set down his mug, glancing back and forth between JJ and me. "What?"

"Well, I think it's important to remember what I

told you about yesterday." I waited for recognition; there was none. "From the ski lift. Tammi and some guy?" I prompted.

"Oh, my God! I completely forgot about that, Libby!" he stood and began pacing the room.

I moved back to the window to watch the young ones.

JJ grew impatient. "Guys, what's this about? What happened?"

I related the story as I recalled the scene. Greg continued to pace, running his fingers through his hair.

Greg stated, "I've got to go talk to Tammi!"

"You indicated that's what you were going to do … you know, when we hung up. You didn't ask her then?"

"No! I got distracted and completely forgot. It was chaos yesterday morning with trying to get the drive plowed, so many people around …" Then he stopped and turned to me. "You know, I *had* gone looking for her when I got stopped by Hector. He was the one who found that Peter had a plow that could be hooked to the front of the Jeep in the garage. I helped him hook it up; that's how we got Peter's driveway plowed."

Something wasn't sitting well with me. "Okay, well, I think we should be careful about how we approach this with her. She's awfully upset about Peter. And I'm hesitant about confronting her. What if the situation wasn't what I thought it was? I could be wrong."

Alexis walked in and saw our concerned faces. "What's going on, guys?"

My head quickly turned to look outside—whew, Joshua and Shadow were still playing. I'd nearly forgotten about them.

JJ said to Greg, "You know that foul play is almost

always connected to those closest to the victim…"

"No one has died!" Greg bellowed.

"Whoa! What's going on?" Alexis settled in on a stool next to her husband at the breakfast bar.

I quickly summed up where we were going with our assumptions about Peter's disappearance. She nodded.

"I agree with Greg. Let's not get ahead of ourselves. Right now, he's only missing," I said.

I poured her a cup of coffee and set it down on the counter. She doctored it with cream and sugar while I pointed to the two outside running rampant across the yard. We could hear yips from Shadow as the blur of black fur blazed by.

Greg settled down. At least he wasn't ready to run out the door and back over to the Schull household immediately. I rubbed his back and planted a kiss on his cheek.

"It's okay, we'll find Peter," I mumbled. "Maybe we could do something else this morning while we wait for the next steps?"

JJ piped up, "Why don't we go skiing?"

Alexis agreed. "Yeah, that was the original plan. And, with all four of us on the slopes, we could keep an eye out for Peter, right? That'd help us feel as though we're contributing somehow."

We all agreed.

* * *

And we weren't the only ones with that idea. We noticed the ski lift lines were filled with familiar faces from the wedding weekend. I recognized all the Schull clan and the Lawsons and Peter's many friends. My heart swelled, recognizing that everyone wanted to find their loved one. There was a part of me that prayed we would find him. However, I realized anyone exposed to the severe elements overnight probably wouldn't have fared well. I certainly hoped that wasn't the case. Like the police said, maybe they'd find him hung over somewhere within the resort village limits.

I saw Abby—today wearing a bright turquoise and purple-colored ski outfit. I looked around for Tammi, but it appeared only one twinsie was out today. That's when I glimpsed a lady who looked familiar, staring at me; she pulled her ski mask down right before the chair got to her, and was lifted up the hill and out of my sight. I couldn't place where I'd seen her before, but assumed it had to be at one of the many parties over the weekend.

We spent hours skiing. Most of Greg's friends scoured the tough runs while we took some easier ones. We intersected with many of them, stopping and comparing notes occasionally.

Peter was nowhere to be found.

Joshua had kept up nicely with his mom and dad most of the morning, but he was getting cranky. We'd done all we could for now. The Johnsons, Greg, and I called it a day.

* * *

To distract Joshua while we made lunch, Alexis asked what type of specialty cake they should order as their prize. I filled Greg in about the contest and how Joshua had won it. All the young boy could talk about was seeing his gingerbread house creation in the front window at Sweet's Sweets.

Alexis and Joshua bantered back and forth; I couldn't help but giggle, listening to ideas from a Gladiator cake to a magical forest theme, complete with dwarves and fairies. I imagined they could replicate any of their ideas at the bakery. The items I'd seen Becky working on the day prior were phenomenal. Samantha and her team appeared to be top-notch, reminding me of some of those on the professional baking shows on cable.

"What flavor is your favorite?" I asked them both.

Together, without hesitation, "Chocolate!"

"Well, at least that's decided!" I laughed. "What about frosting?"

"Chocolate!" Again, was the resounding decision.

Once we had finished our chili cheese dogs, Alexis coaxed Joshua to lie down with her and watch a movie. He was out within minutes.

JJ and Greg headed over to the Schulls'. He was eager to find his friend and couldn't quite settle down, only hanging around the house. JJ was eager to get to know his friends better as well. My guess was that JJ's detective brain wanted to get in on the action.

I used the opportunity for my turn taking a hot bubble bath to ease the aching muscles. Not long after that, I snuggled up with a fuzzy blanket in an oversized chair next to the fireplace in our suite and read my book until I dozed off with Shadow at my feet.

* * *

The sun was low on the horizon when I woke. I found Alexis in the kitchen heating the tea kettle and the bakery box sat open on the countertop.

"Where's Joshua?" I asked.

"Playroom," she stated, only she looked upset. "Libby, something happened at Sweet's Sweets."

"What do you mean?"

"I called to place our cake order. Joshua woke up from his nap pestering me about going to see the gingerbread house in the front window *right now*," she chuckled. "Anyway, she shared with me that there was vandalism."

"What?" Shocked, it was surprising to hear something like that happening in this small ski resort town.

"Yeah. Her beautiful shop. Can't imagine who would vandalize a bakery."

The kettle whistled, and she poured boiling water into two mugs. Pulling out two small plates from the cabinet, she continued, "Samantha wasn't pleased, of course. Normally, she explained, they could have finished our cake within a day, but she was so apologetic when she had to push our order out until Tuesday afternoon."

"Well, that's understandable. I wouldn't have expected to have it within a day anyway, would you?"

"No! I'm sure there's a lot that goes into creating something like that. Design, construction, and then with all their normal day-to-day customers ... sheesh!"

"By the way, what design did you and Joshua settle on?"

"The magical forest."

That was my pick too; not that I had a say in it.

We sat at the breakfast bar, enjoying a sweet treat from the bakery box as a late afternoon snack. I filled Alexis in on the drama over at the Schull household. More particularly, I needed to vent about Tammi. I knew my best friend would understand the insecure feelings. Alexis was a brilliant listener. When I got to the part about what I'd seen from the ski lift, she finally reacted.

"I know you, Libby. You aren't the type of person who makes stuff up—gossiping about unfounded rumors. I trust that what you saw *was* something. You told Greg, right?"

"Yeah. That was weird, too. He reacted strongly, then forgot to ask Tammi about it. I assumed that's what he's planned to do this afternoon. We'll see." I took another bite, savoring the brownie. Sweet's Sweets were so amazing!

"What do you mean, 'he reacted strongly'?"

"He caught himself, but he nearly called her a nasty name. Seemed like he wasn't all that surprised, though. Maybe this isn't out of character for her. Who knows?"

"Oh, that would be a big deal for him. I don't recall hearing him cuss much, and especially disparaging a woman? No, that's not our Greg. This woman must have done a number on him."

I agreed, laughing when imaging the two together in high school. "I've heard him say a few choice words when he stubbed a toe once, but you're right, nothing like calling people names." It was out of character for him, which led me to believe that she'd cheated on him or something hurtful. "*Who* cheats on their spouse on their wedding day … or weekend?" I added.

"Reportedly, Prince Charles," she laughed. "No, seriously. I don't understand it either." She hesitated; her expression turned grim. "Wait. Libby, are you thinking what I'm thinking?"

"What's that?"

"Are you considering the possibility that Tammi has something to do with Peter's disappearance?"

I nodded my head. "I don't think it's out of the realm

of possibilities, do you?"

"Well, no. Cheating is one thing … it doesn't necessarily link to anything more sinister."

"True. And we honestly don't know if Peter wandered off willingly." I wondered if that was true, especially since his phone was found back at the house.

"Again, *who* does this on their wedding weekend? With all their family and friends in town?" She had a good point.

The front door opened. We heard the guys chatting away as they shed their winter layers in the foyer.

Greg walked right over to me and planted a kiss. He appeared serious, though. My eyes formed the question. He shrugged, then said, "She hasn't changed a bit."

"So, you confronted her about what I told you?" I asked.

JJ and Alexis stood across the counter from us, waiting to learn the story.

"Oh yeah. She totally denies it—says you're the jealous girlfriend."

I jumped up. "I did *not* make it up!" Then, turned the question around. "Wait, what do I have to be jealous about? I haven't accused her of being with *you* on the slopes. I don't understand."

He held his hands up in surrender. "Gaslighting," he simply stated. "Hey, don't worry! I believe you, Libs."

"So why does it feel as though you don't?"

"I believe you saw something. Also, I think it's true that *she* hasn't changed her dramatic, manipulative ways."

"Thank you," I said, as calmly as I could muster. I also started to question myself. "I *swear* it was her. I mean, who else has such a recognizable ski outfit? Right?"

He stood, walked over, and pulled me into his arms. "I

hear you. And, really, it's not our business."

"What if it is related to Peter's disappearance, though?" I pointed out.

He nodded slowly. "How about we'll worry about that if he doesn't turn up? He's *going* to show up here shortly. Either someone will find him, out and about having fun, or ..."

I understood. He didn't want to consider the alternative.

His phone chimed. He released his arms from around me and reached into his jeans' pockets.

"It's my mom," he said, as he walked from the room to answer.

When he came back in, he asked who'd be interested in joining them for dinner at their place. We were all in agreement.

CHAPTER THIRTEEN

Tuesday rolled around and there was still no sighting of Peter. We were now beyond the 48-hour point—in harsh conditions on the mountain. We continued to pray that wasn't where he was. The question was—if not there, where?

Most of the guests left town Tuesday as they had already planned. Of course, Peter's family still gathered with police and SAR. They also recruited their influential friends, undoubtedly to gain better resources. Even Bill now admitted this was too long for Peter to have been out of touch.

After taking Shadow for a walk around the little community, I headed to the kitchen and filled a mug of coffee. JJ was reading on his tablet in the corner. No sign of Joshua or Lexi from their suite yet. Greg had already left for the Schull's place.

JJ looked up. "Greg's family seems nice," he simply stated.

I nodded and grinned. "They really are, aren't they?" I sat down on the sofa and carefully took a sip from my mug.

"Bill talked a little about Peter and Michael's business. Apparently, there are several foreign companies with similar technology now. MedDyno, when it was a startup twenty years ago, manufactured a one-of-a-kind device. Of course, they patented it, but that doesn't keep others from improving upon the technology and presenting their own version." JJ set his coffee mug on the counter.

"And you think it's possible this has hurt business recently?" I asked. He nodded, but there was more I was reading into his posture. "Wait, what, do you think a competitor kidnapped him on his wedding day? For what, a hostile takeover or something?" I laughed. Seemed absurd to me.

He shrugged and took a sip of his coffee. "The other issue at hand is that the FDA is investigating several recent safety issues. Bill seems to think the 'boys' went cheap. Something about cheap China parts. So, are they in bed with China?"

All that was over my head, but it certainly could be a motive. Then again, we weren't even certain that Peter was truly missing. It'd only been a couple of days.

"Why Peter? He's the sales guy, but Michael and Raj certainly have the same, if not more, at stake in the company. Wasn't Michael the inventor?"

"That's right. And that's why I haven't fully bought into the theory that Peter's disappearance is business related."

Lexi walked into the kitchen while we were talking. She

opened the refrigerator, then turned to us. "Anyone up for breakfast in town today? We don't want to cook every meal while on vacation, do we?"

JJ smiled as his beautiful wife walked toward him, leaned down, and kissed him. "We probably should try out the places the ladies suggested the other day," he muttered after her soft kiss.

I agreed. I called Greg to see if he would join, and he told us to go ahead without him. He felt he should stick around, but he sent me several pictures of Peter. He had a good idea—we could ask around at the businesses we visited. Maybe someone would recognize him. I noticed one photo was one from the wedding night—him and Tammi.

The entire plan went south once I let Shadow out to do her business in the yard. I watched the whole thing happen from the living room windows. A skunk crossed her path. She chased it, and then the rest of our morning was shot. We all went into panic mode—JJ quickly looked up suggestions online for how to deal with skunk; Lexi and I rummaged through the home for supplies; poor freezing Shadow stood at the back door, staring at us to let her in. Thankfully, the skunk hadn't stuck around; it hightailed it out of the yard.

To avoid getting the skunk smell in the house, I put on the oldest clothing I brought, went outside and walked Shadow around front and over to the garage. Opening the service door, I could already tell it was warmer. Other than a utility vehicle and some outdoor tools hanging in holders on the way, there wasn't much else in the garage. There was space inside, near the door to get out of the elements and pull the hose in where I could spray her down. It was the best we could do in the situation. Lexi offered to help, but

I thought it'd be best to have the least number of people exposed to the horrific odor.

After what felt like hours, using apple cider vinegar, baking soda, over and over, I had the others smell her to see if it was any better. The overwhelming stench overloaded my senses.

Out on the front patio, Lexi took a sniff. "I mean, it's not *horrible*. But there's still an odor."

"What are we going to do? I have to get this poor girl warm. It's freezing out here!"

"I think she's good enough to bring her inside. Maybe try this again now in the shower with warm water?" JJ suggested.

I agreed with that and got in the shower with her. A nice hot shower. We both shivered until the room filled with steam. I continued making a paste with the baking soda and then worked in through her coat methodically. I even tried finishing with some of my shampoo.

"It's better," Alexis said when we got out.

I dried her off as well as I could in the bathroom, but I couldn't get that stink out of my head. It wasn't good enough; we had to do more.

"There's a groomer there in the Plaza. I saw it the other day—can you look it up, JJ? Maybe they can help—certainly they are more suited for this than we are, right?"

He found the number for Puppy Chic. I called and explained the situation, and they said they had just the thing to help.

We loaded up in my vehicle. It didn't take long before all the windows came down, but we turned the heater up full blast to compensate.

* * *

Fifteen minutes later, a lady probably somewhere around my age ushered us into a backroom. There were two small dogs in crates, yipping as we entered the room. They sort of reminded me of the cute fluff balls we met in Jerome recently. Except, I believe these were Shih Tzu, if I wasn't mistaken. They all have a similar fluffy look to them.

The woman introduced herself as Kelly Sweet-Porter. She walked us over to one of the wash stalls for large dogs.

She bent down and lifted Shadow's chin, cooing to her, "Well, you must have had fun chasing that skunk, huh?" Then she looked up at me. "Smells like you did a great job already. Could be far worse."

"Oh, it *was* far worse a couple of hours ago. There's no way we could have been in a car with her."

"Okay, well, this really won't take very long. There's a bakery next door—highly recommended," she started, her eyes cast down sheepishly. "It's my mom's place," she admitted.

"Oh! You're Samantha's daughter!"

"So, you've already been over there?"

"Yes! The other day, we joined the baking contest. Actually, my friend and her son won the contest." I pointed outside; they had already headed over to the bakery. "We're going to pick up their cake while we're in town."

She looked hesitant. "Uh. There was a lot of damage. I was there yesterday helping mom clean up."

"Any idea who did it?"

She shook her head.

"Well, my friends are over there now. I'll join them, and then you'll call or text me when she's ready?"

"Yep, got your number here. I'll text." She turned back to Shadow, who was skulking away from her already.

"Oh, I know, girl, you've already had enough today, huh?" she ruffled up her fur, talking in a sweet voice. To me she said, "Shouldn't be more than an hour. I like to leave the product on and set for twenty minutes. Then we rinse and repeat. It won't be long."

I walked out the front door this time and over to the bakery next door. Now, from this side of the building, I saw that Sweet's Sweets had plywood over the front window. My heart sank.

JJ, Alexis, and Samantha had apparently been placating the child, who obviously had been crying. Using cookies, Sam clearly persuaded him to stop crying. His hands and face—they were covered in blue frosting.

"Someone stole the gingerbread house," she explained.

"What?!" I gasped.

"Vandalism and theft," Samantha said, standing up and shaking her head. "I don't understand it. Why the bakery?"

I looked around and saw that they'd cleaned up, but Sam's shop had lost its magic without light shining through the front window. Without the cute displays. Even her bakery case was nearly barren. She saw that I'd noticed.

"A couple of us baked yesterday to fill orders; the others cleaned. My husband, Beau, got the windows covered before nightfall. As you can tell, we're still losing heat, and it could be a couple days before it's replaced."

JJ asked, "Any idea who'd do this? Disgruntled employee?"

"No, I can't even imagine. My employees have been with me for years now—we're a family. And if you saw their faces yesterday morning when they walked in, you'd know immediately it wasn't an inside job."

"Upset customer?"

She slowly made her way behind the counter. "We get favorable reviews and I can't recall the last time someone complained about anything."

Becky came through with a tray of croissants, which she carefully inserted into the case. "Good morning! Oh, is it still morning?" she looked at her watch. Eleven-thirty. "Close enough. Good to see you guys again. I am nearly finished with your cake; only a few more touches," she winked.

Samantha smiled. "Oh, right! You guys are here for your cake—and here I am, bending your ear about our break-in."

I waved it off. "Actually, we dropped Shadow off next door." I pointed that direction and made a face. "Skunk. While we wait for her to be cleaned up, we thought we'd take Nancy's suggestion for lunch and go to Michael's Kitchen. Maybe we can grab the cake on the way out of town instead?"

"Sure, sure. No problem. Glad you stopped in to say hi, though." She looked at Joshua, who was still making a mess of the cookie. She chuckled. "I'm so sorry about your gingerbread house, little man." She told Joshua that so many people had stopped in to say how much they loved his gingerbread house while it was displayed for the one day. I was sure she exaggerated the number, but she was so sweet. Lexi wiped his face and we let Sam know we'd be back soon.

As we loaded into the 4Runner, leaving the windows down because of the smell, a little voice sounded. "But, why couldn't we get the cake now, Mom?"

"Honey, they weren't quite done."

He looked disappointed for a moment, but then his

eyes lit up. "I can't wait to see it!"

"I know—but let's go eat some lunch first."

We cranked up the heat again for the short drive.

* * *

Nancy had been right. Lunch was delicious. We familiarized ourselves with the town by driving around and searching for the other places the ladies previously mentioned. We still had four more days and wanted to see as much as we could.

My phone chimed. It was Kelly; Shadow was ready to be picked up.

While we made our way back to the Plaza, an image of the cranky lady came back to me. I remembered how angry she was the day of the baking contest, and how out of place it was. Could she have vandalized the bakery? Seemed extreme to me. What for? Because a boy won the grand prize instead of her? That seemed ludicrous.

I walked up to the register at Puppy Chic and paid. A girl at the front desk went to get Shadow and when she walked her out, Kelly was trailing behind.

"She did so great!" Kelly exclaimed. "And, I believe, all skunk scent is gone now!"

That was the best news of the day. My phone chimed again. It was Greg wondering when we'd be back. That reminded me of the photos.

"Hey, Kelly … I know this is a longshot, but we have a friend that went missing a couple days ago." I held up my phone. "Here are a few photos. You haven't seen this guy around town, have you?"

She gasped. "What the heck?"

"You've seen Peter? Do you know him?" I asked.

Her eyes widened, and she pointed at my screen. "Tammi is back in town?"

CHAPTER FOURTEEN

Y ou know them?" I asked, stunned that Kelly recognized the photo.

"I know her. I used to work with Tammi," she explained.

"Here?"

"No, this was years back. She was married to this guy—um, not *him*," she pointed to the photo again. "Oh, what was his name? Um, something Chavez … Jorge, I believe."

"You looked surprised that she was back in town."

"After she took Jorge for a ride … well, I wouldn't show my face in the same small town again!"

"What happened? If you don't mind my asking…"

"Oh wow, that's a long story. I was super relieved when she left Taos, that's for sure." She glanced around the room. The girl at the register was helping another customer. "Listen, I have to get back to work now. I have your number; maybe we could talk later."

"Sounds good. Thanks, Kelly, for taking care of Shadow."

She turned, about to enter the back room, and looked back. "Hey, tell my mom to send over some donuts when she gets a chance!" she said, laughing.

I giggled. "Will do!"

* * *

Joshua put his hands over his mouth. His eyes were wide and sparkling.

"Sam! This is precisely what I described to you on the phone!" Lexi said elatedly. "How…?"

The magical forest cake was outstanding. The chocolate sheet cake rested on a wooden platform. I assumed that was for stability since the design grew upward from there. Realistic foot-tall trees lined the forest, among rolling hills. Under the canopy of the forest, there were adorable thatched roofed cottages … hobbit-like homes! Dwarves were busy working throughout their little village. I had no idea how they'd made them look so realistic; the detail was amazing. Then I spotted two fairies in the trees, looking down upon the hustling dwarves.

"Oh, it wasn't me. This one was all Becky—isn't she talented?" Sam called out toward the backroom.

All of us stood nodding our heads. Becky came through the doorway and saw our pleased expressions.

"This was the most fun I've had on a cake in a long time. Thank you for the great idea!"

Alexis pointed down at her son. "It's all him…"

Sam and Becky both commented about what a creative little boy he was. He smiled proudly.

While they were talking, I leaned into JJ and whispered, "How do you suppose this is getting home in one piece?"

He stood admiring the work of art and slowly shrugged his shoulders. "With your driving? I do not know." He laughed, and I gave him a soft slug on his arm.

Outside, JJ and Becky made it all work, placing it securely in the back of the 4Runner. I went back into the shop to thank Samantha again. Kelly was talking to her when I opened the door.

"Hello again," she called out to me. "Got that masterpiece road ready, did you?"

Sam interrupted. "Libby, my daughter was telling me that one of your friends is missing?"

"Yeah." I pulled my phone from my pocket and showed her the picture. "Greg's friend from college."

Kelly and Sam exchanged glances.

"What? Have you seen him?"

Sam cleared her throat. "No. Kelly was telling me that Tammi was back in town. I was praying it wasn't true, but now, I see it is. That girl is trouble," she said, pointing at my phone.

I nodded. "Yeah, Kelly mentioned before that they worked together." I saw Sam's gaze move to the front window, now boarded up. "Wait. Are you thinking she's responsible for this?"

"She was a pistol when she lived here. Took exception with many people in town, actually. Can't say for sure she had a vendetta against our family, but then again, who knows? I'm surprised to learn she'd showed her face anywhere near here. And, you said she's the one marrying your missing friend?"

I nodded. "Yeah, already married, actually."

Sam and Kelly once again signaled silently to one another. Then, Sam came around the counter and put her hand on my shoulder. "I really hope you find the missing groom. I know the authorities are already working on finding him, but if there's anything we can do, please let us know."

My heart melted. These two ladies were so kind. I reached out to hug Sam, and then Kelly, too. "You've filed a police report for your vandalism, right?"

"Yep," Sam nodded. "Oh, and real quick. Could you send me that picture with the two of them? We'll keep our eyes out in town. And where did you say they're staying … a resort?"

"Peter owns a home here—on Spruce Lane. Gargantuan mansion."

"I think I know just the one you're talking about. Watched that one being built several years back."

"Mom used to break into houses for a living," Kelly blurted out. When she saw my jaw drop, she clarified. "Oh, all legal, don't worry. It was a USDA job—she'd go in and clean up places after foreclosure. When keys weren't available, she got pretty good at breaking in."

I laughed at the image of this amiable middle-aged lady picking a lock, or potentially climbing through a window.

My phone rang; it was Greg.

"Sorry, I've got to get this." I turned away and answered.

When I hung up, the ladies sensed from my reaction, it wasn't good news.

"They found his body," I simply stated. I looked out the front door; Alexis and JJ were standing there talking to Becky. Joshua was already in his car seat; JJ was holding Shadow on her leash. "Oh boy, I'm sorry ladies, but we've got to run."

Kelly whispered as she hugged me goodbye, "Have the police looked into Tammi's past?" I pulled back, looking at her questioningly. She shrugged, then added, "I'm just saying … it might be a good idea."

With that, I said goodbye and went outside to deliver the grim news to my friends.

Dark clouds loomed ahead as we carefully made our way up the mountain's winding roads and back to our house with the cake intact.

* * *

Greg was sitting by the fire, intently focused on his phone, when we walked in. JJ asked for his help with his son's prize. They carefully walked it in and displayed it front and center at the breakfast bar.

"What happened to Peter?" I finally asked, once Joshua had run off to the playroom.

"They found him in the backcountry. Sounds like accidental death, but that's not official or anything."

"So, he went off-trail skiing then? Alone?"

"Well, I think that's what's being determined. It's strange he would have gone off alone. Usually, an outfitter's group would take you to this area. It's not open to the public, and it's not part of the resort, from what I understand. Probably the reason ski patrol wouldn't have searched there."

"Ohhh," I managed to get out. What words were left to say? My mind whirled as I remembered how Peter had been skiing with his friends earlier that day he went missing. Wouldn't they have gone with him? Yet no one had mentioned anything about that. "So, what's next?" I asked. "His poor parents."

"Yeah, they're pretty broken up."

"And Tammi…" I whispered, thinking of Kelly's earlier warning.

"You can imagine how distraught she must be. Apparently, they're preparing to head back to Albuquerque. Peter's body has been transported to a morgue there already."

"Wow, I cannot believe any of this," I said, sinking down onto the couch.

Alexis sat down next to Greg. "What can we do?"

He shrugged. What was there to do?

Breaking the silence, I filled him in on our earlier conversations with Sam and Kelly while we were at the bakery. Not that it was much, only I found it interesting how they knew Tammi. Greg hadn't known previously that Tammi had lived in Taos.

I turned to Greg with an idea. "Do you think Tammi would talk to me? Maybe we should go over there."

His eyebrows furrowed, looking pointedly at me. "Um, I don't know. Why? Libby, you aren't thinking …"

"I'd like to look around a bit—maybe ask a question or two? That's all."

"Libby…" his voice trailed off.

"It'll be okay. I promise." I held up my fingers, giving the recognizable scout's honor. When I looked over at Alexis and JJ, I saw their skepticism as well. "Oh, c'mon guys. There has to be more to this, don't you think?"

JJ spoke up first. "Leave it to the authorities, Libby."

"Of course. But what will it hurt to help them along?"

They knew they wouldn't win once I had my mind set on something. JJ and Greg went to retrieve their coats. Alexis said she'd stay with Joshua and would come up with an evening meal plan. I grabbed Shadow's leash and bundled myself up. The three of us loaded into the 4Runner and headed over to Peter's place.

CHAPTER FIFTEEN

There were considerably fewer cars around as we drove up the lane and pulled into the circular driveway. Even so, with all the vehicles owned by Peter alone, you'd have thought the party continued. We parked behind a tan colored Hummer I hadn't seen there before.

"So, what exactly is it you're looking for, Libby?"

"I'm not sure. You'd think someone knows *something*. A minor detail that explains who Peter was with when he left on this expedition … or, oh, I don't know. But there has to be some explanation. Why wouldn't his friends, or family, know that he headed off for backcountry skiing?"

"Because he was Peter … those are the things he'd do!" Greg exclaimed.

"Okay, yes. But even you said earlier that it was

surprising on his wedding weekend to run off."

He shook his head and then pointed with his hand for me to lead the way. JJ also followed dutifully.

The closer we got to the front door, I whispered to the guys. "If I could get into the master suite somehow *without* Tammi ... you know, she's been holed up in there for days. What was she up to?"

"Oh, for heaven's sake, Libby. She was distraught, wondering about the welfare of her new husband."

"I know. I know. But, after what I explained earlier ... what Kelly told me, I feel we need to dig into her background story."

"*We?*" JJ interjected.

"Okay, the police need to look more closely at her, but perhaps we can provide some assistance."

Greg knocked at the door, as he also opened it. "Hello!" he hollered out, pushing the door further and stepping in. "Hi, it's Greg. Mr. or Mrs. Schull—are you here?"

Raj poked his head around the corner, coming from the kitchen. "In here, Greg," he said, his voice somber.

We all followed Greg. Shadow's hind-end wiggled wildly as Raj bent over to pet her. He gave me a hug and shook JJ's hand as well. Sitting at the breakfast bar was Hector, who offered us beers. They explained that Peter's family followed the coroner, who'd already taken Peter's body to Albuquerque for the autopsy. Most guests had headed out earlier as well.

"Oh, I'm so sorry about your loss," I said to Peter's friends. "It's so shocking; I can't imagine what you all are going through."

Both of them bowed their heads slightly, nodding. Then, I caught the glance between Raj and Hector.

"Wait, have you guys learned something new?" I asked.

"And, where's Tammi?"

They each nervously took swigs from their bottles.

"Tammi left a while ago—said she had to get out; something about an errand to run in Taos." Then Raj proceeded, his serious tone palpable. "Greg, how well have you kept in contact with Peter over the years?"

"We spoke a couple times a year, if that. He was a busy man."

"Yeah, that's about what I thought … so, you don't truly know what's going on within the company then."

"He hadn't really mentioned much work-wise, no."

Raj proceeded to tell us about several lawsuits related to product quality. There was a whistleblower who'd come forward over a year ago with astonishing claims accusing MedDyno of killing patients. The FDA got involved and the company's lawyers were fighting the claims.

"I'm sorry, I'm not entirely sure exactly what the company manufactures … what does this medical device *do*?" I asked.

"Oh! Right. Michael patented a way for diabetics to manage blood sugar without injections. In fact, they don't even have to prick their finger any longer for blood tests. It has been a game-changer." Raj enthusiastically explained to us how the device was implanted and the basic logistics of its inner workings. It sounded clever, even though I didn't fully understand how it actually accomplished what they claim.

"Wow. That sounds ingenious. So, what's gone wrong recently to bring on a lawsuit?" Greg asked.

Raj corrected, "*Lawsuits…*" He took a swig of beer and set the bottle on the countertop. "Peter and Michael have been vigilantly trying to figure that out. Both of them have parked themselves in the quality control area at our manufacturing plant for months, overseeing operations."

"Because the device has been successful for many years now, right?" I was curious. From all the conversations over the past few days, it sounded as though the company had been extremely successful.

"Definitely. It was shocking to learn how many people had died. The thing is … had they actually died from complications from diabetes, or a malfunction in our product? The device only detects blood sugar levels, then automatically dispenses the proper amount of insulin in response. It doesn't *cure* diabetes, which, as you know, comes with a host of complications. The claimants accuse that the device over-medicated patients. Also, in certain instances, under-medicated patients which also allegedly caused problems."

"And your company thinks that's incorrect?" Greg asked.

Hector spoke up. "Greg, our engineers and the quality control testers have thoroughly reviewed the device, and there has been *no sign* that the product has malfunctioned." He pulled out a phone from his back pocket. "You see here…" he opened an app, typed in a username and password, and finished with a facial recognition step. We all looked over his shoulders to see the screen.

"Is this data from an actual patient?" I wanted to know.

"Well, yes, but it's test data. During the trials, we monitored diabetic volunteers, as did our house physicians and researchers. Otherwise, actual patients who have now purchased our product, their results go directly to their own doctors. Privacy is of utmost importance—you know, HIPAA laws—so they built all that into the app."

I was skeptical. Seemed particularly invasive and ripe for … what, fraud maybe? But, what could someone actually gain by accidentally accessing someone's blood sugar level information? I wasn't sure.

He ran through several screens, explaining things that were way over my head. The gist of it, though, made sense. A doctor refers the patient as a candidate. They implant the device in their arm near a primary artery, and the doctor monitors via the app. This way, the doctor has up-to-the-minute data about their patient and can help regulate dosages. The patient also has oversight as well.

That explanation made me even more leery. "So, let me see if I have this right. The doctor gets an alert that someone's blood sugar is high, or low, and they adjust the dosage through the app?"

"Yep. But, keep in mind, the dosage adjustments would only be required if the readings *over time* warranted it, or as an emergency alert potentially. The doctor doesn't continuously monitor; they have way too many patients to do that. But, conversely, if the patient has a concern, they can call the doctor for consultation without necessarily going into their office. Instead, they would handle it, um, well, kind of like tele-health. Saves both the doctor and patient time."

"Wow. I had no idea." I looked at Greg, astonished by what we were learning. Then I remembered why we were actually here: Peter's death. "So, are you guys thinking somehow the company's lawsuit could have something to do with what happened to Peter?"

Raj hesitated slightly before answering, then sighed. "We don't know anything actually, Libby. However, what we were discussing when you arrived … well, Hector mentioned Michael's reaction to the lawsuit."

"How do you mean?" I asked.

Hector jumped in. "He's been super nervous. Actually, angry ... we've never seen him that way. He's always been a calm, introverted, nerdy science guy. Lately, he's been fiery, angry, and not like himself at all."

Greg nodded. "You're right, that doesn't sound like Michael. He hasn't been that way this weekend, though."

"Exactly. He's been great this weekend. But over the past year, maybe longer, he's changed so much. We were wondering if that had to do with the lawsuit. It wouldn't be surprising—the company is his baby. I mean, for all of us, it's a high-stress situation, regardless."

Not following exactly, I asked, "Do you think Michael had something to do with Peter's accident?"

Hector was quick to answer. "If it was an accident, then no. I think we're questioning whether it really was an accident."

"Oh. What do you think happened then?"

"Honestly, Libby, we don't know. Peter was such a force—very much living his best life. He was a specimen of health ... and everyone loved him. It doesn't make sense that he's gone now."

"But a skiing accident ... that can happen and doesn't have anything to do with someone's health necessarily. What exactly is your concern?"

Raj straightened in his seat. "Oh! Sorry. We learned earlier from the sheriff's office that he died of hypothermia. Of course, they're waiting for a final autopsy, so that's preliminary. From what they told the family so far, there was no obvious sign of trauma consistent with skiing—like running into a tree or off a cliff, as an example." He took another swig of beer and turned pointedly to Greg. "As I'm sure you're aware, Peter's an adventurer, an extreme outdoorsman. It simply doesn't make sense that he put himself in a situation that exposed him to the elements like that. Something else happened up there on the mountain and we're determined to figure out what."

I let that sink in for a moment. JJ and Greg continued bantering theories with the guys and my mind went straight to Tammi. I was certain I'd seen her with another man—*was that person 'what happened on the mountain'? Who was she with on the ski hill?*

We'd been talking with the guys for close to an hour. If I was going to snoop, I'd need to get a move on; she could arrive home anytime. I excused myself to find the restroom. As soon as I got up from my stool, Shadow leapt up and followed me.

Walking down the expansive hallway, we passed several doors before arriving at the restroom. I looked behind me. No one was around, so I continued along to the end of the corridor and found Tammi and Peter's bedroom. The door was open. Shadow traipsed on in.

"Tammi?" I called out. No answer.

Housekeeping hadn't been there yet; it appeared as though Tammi had been hurriedly packing—clothes were everywhere. I looked around at the mess. Articles of clothing were partially inside the large pink suitcase, but also littered from the closet to where the suitcase resided on the bed.

What precisely was I looking for? I wasn't sure, but I was determined to figure out if Peter's friends were right. *Was Peter's death intentional or accidental?* I glanced around the room, easily determining which bedside table was his versus Tammi's. Tiptoeing around the random t-shirt, pants, and a robe on the floor along the way, I sat down on his side of the bed. I reached for the nightstand drawer, simultaneously looking behind me, expecting to be caught at any moment.

The top drawer had only a few predictable items: ChapStick, tissues, an extra phone charger, and some antacids. I went for the second of the three drawers. In here, there were a couple sci-fi novels and a notepad. I pulled out the pad. Thumbing through the pages, it appeared to be business notes. Seemed to be a lot of MedDyno tech speak of which I didn't understand. Something written on a small blue Post-It caught my eye. It read: **memujidupe**. Interesting, but meant absolutely nothing to me. Still, I slipped it in my pocket and kept reading through the notebook pages until I came to the newest writings; absolutely no clues. What had I expected? A note that said, 'if found dead, this is who killed me'. I mean, c'mon. It's never that easy!

I opened the third drawer and found some slippers that apparently came from a resort they'd visited. Clearly, the nightstand was not where I'd find the secrets. Unless Tammi's held better loot. I moved around the bed and started rifling around in her drawers. Similar personal items were in the top one, along with a selection of books and some nighttime cough medicine. Neither of the other two drawers held anything of significance.

Shadow was still busy sniffing all around, examining each corner of the room. Standing up, I scanned the rest of the large suite and decided not to dive into their clothes drawers.

Meanwhile, my pup had gone into the closet and I

heard a little whimper. I followed and gawked at what I found. Their closet was the size of an entire bedroom. It was immaculate. His side with all his outdoorsy-type clothing hung with color-coded precision. Racks of boots and shoes. No business attire anywhere. On her side, similar with the outdoors-wear, but she also had several hangers with fancy cocktail dresses. Shadow was at the far end, sitting and pointing her nose upward. It appeared she was interested in a beautiful shelving unit displaying Tammi's shoes. Upon closer inspection, I found myself slightly envious of the choices in footwear this lady had. I picked up an exquisite pair—and read the label inside: Manolo Blahnik. I've never been a shoe person, or a fashion connoisseur, but I was an avid viewer of *Sex and the City* and a super fan of Carrie Bradshaw. It was easy to recognize the expensive shoes immediately. Holding them in my hand, I swore I could smell money.

I went to set them back in place and saw a faint circular outline on the shelf where I was about to set the shoe. My finger gently touched it, moving along the indentation, wondering why it was there. Did it somehow hold the shoes in place, like a magnet or something? As I circled it again, I must have pushed down slightly. It gave a little—it was a type of button. I pushed harder, and it made a noise; the wall slid to the left. I quickly threw the shoes back in their place before the shelf disappeared behind a wall.

Shadow's ears perked curiously, her nose twitching, reaching into the darkness of the newly discovered room. I nervously stared ahead, wondering what awaited us. Shadow went in first; I followed. As soon as we crossed the threshold, a motion-sensor triggered soft blue lighting. It gradually illuminated the space that was approximately eight feet by eight feet. There was a huge steel safe taller than Greg, the type with the double step doors. It had a keypad and what looked like a ship's steering wheel that had to be navigated before entering. *What were they hiding in there?*

Across from that monstrosity, there was another fairly large one built right into the wall. Underneath the wall safe, and along the floor, were various file cabinets. I tried to open two drawers and found them locked.

Something sounded from behind me. I spun around. Voices were coming our way.

"C'mon, Shadow," I whispered. "Let's go."

She ignored me and kept sniffing along the base of the giant safe.

"Shadow! Now!" I hissed more urgently. She came.

We hustled over the threshold, back into the closet. The secret room's lighting gradually dimmed. My eyes darted all around, trying to find how to close the door. A few seconds after the room darkened, the sliding wall automatically closed. *How cool is that?*

The voices were getting closer, so I swiftly directed Shadow into the bedroom and toward the hallway. As I stepped out into the hallway, Raj gave an inquisitive look.

"Whatcha doing in there, Libby?"

I looked down at Shadow and gave a quick snort. "She's always running off snooping around. Guess she found Peter's room!" I laughed, feeling only slightly guilty for blaming the dog.

Hector came out of a doorway a couple of doors down from where we were standing.

"Here it is!" he held up a phone charger in victory.

Before he also started questioning what I was doing

this far down the hallway, I asked, "Are you guys staying here now that everyone's left?" It seemed that was the case since he'd come from one of the guest rooms.

In unison, they both said yes. Then Raj explained how they'd need to gather all the work-related equipment and files from Peter's house and move them back to the office in Albuquerque. They'd stay another couple of days. Instead of continuing to pay for their vacation rental, the family was gracious to allow them to stay at the house.

We emerged into the great room and I caught the look from Greg indicating he was sorry he couldn't keep them away longer. I gave him a slight smile. Raj and Hector got the charger hooked up and then continued showing Greg photos on Hector's phone.

"I'm going to take Shadow outside … it's been a while." They barely looked up as we slipped out the front door.

The late afternoon shadows cast a chill through me. We walked west to find some remnants of sun. Shadow's nose immediately went into overdrive. She twisted and turned about, trying to decide which way to go. Toward the garage, she pulled aggressively at the leash, nearly sending me tripping over some railroad ties outlining a dormant flower bed.

"Whoa! Where are you going, girl?"

I struggled to keep up, jogging along to avoid having the leash pulled from my hand. She rounded the garage and abruptly stopped at the back corner. I could see off into the distance where skiers swooshed down the hill at rapid speed. Shadow wasn't intent on them, though; her paws were furiously digging at the ground about ten feet away from the back wall of the garage. I tried pulling her back, but she was insistent. Curious, I kneeled down nearby, inspecting the frozen ground she was working on. It was so frozen over; she wasn't making much headway. Figuring she was after some critter, I pulled her away and we continued out into the woods toward the ski hill.

There was a movement in the trees behind us. I spun around, praying not to face a wild animal. From fifty feet away, I glimpsed pink. Someone was running away from the property, heading east, away from the ski area. Shadow heard the rustling and barked, lunging that direction. We took off, only coming to a stop when we reached the next property, where the terrain immediately dropped off into a steep canyon. We lost the person and I couldn't figure out where they could have possibly gone.

Leading Shadow to the front of a three-story log cabin, I looked around for any sign of life. The property appeared to be vacated—whether only a vacation rental, or the people weren't currently home, I couldn't tell. We made our way to the road and walked down the winding lane until we found Peter's home again.

"You were gone quite a while," Greg expressed concern as we came in, breathless.

"Someone was out in the woods behind the house. She ran off when she saw us."

"She?"

"Yeah. I assumed. The person was wearing pink."

Greg turned to the guys. "Abby already left town, right?"

I grinned, realizing we both were thinking along the same line. Abby and Tammi had worn those bright pink ski outfits the other day. I wasn't so sure that was the same pink I'd seen today, even so, good thought.

Raj nodded, "Yeah, I think so."

I shrugged. "Well, that was strange. I'm not sure why someone would run off like that unless they were up to no good. Anyway, they're gone now." I turned to Greg and JJ. "Shall we?"

"Yep. Let's get back to our place," Greg said, and JJ nodded.

"Y'all still vacationing here the rest of the week?" Hector asked Greg.

"Yeah. We'll stay and finish the vacation with our friends," Greg nodded toward JJ. "I imagine there won't be a service for at least several days, if not a week, right?"

"Hmmm, haven't heard. I'd expect that's about right, though," Raj answered.

Greg embraced Raj, then added, "Hey man, we'd love to have you guys over for meals. Or maybe we can all grab something in town, since you'll be here a while longer."

Both Hector and Raj agreed they'd be in touch, and we all said our goodbyes.

CHAPTER SIXTEEN

Before we made it back to the house, my phone chimed. It was a text from Kelly.

Stop by Sweet's Sweets if you're in town this week. Have some information I've left with my mom.

"That's interesting," I turned in my seat looking at JJ. "Kelly—Samantha's daughter from Sweet's Sweets just texted me. Says she has some information. Wonder what that's about?"

"Call her," he said matter-of-factly.

I sat for a second, wondering whether I really wanted to get into another conversation at the moment. I wanted time alone with Greg to talk through my findings over at Peter's house. But, I supposed JJ was right. A quick phone call could clear up the lingering curiosity.

I tapped the call symbol on the text message, listening for the familiar ringing sound. Kelly picked up almost immediately, leaving me with no time to change my mind.

"Libby! So happy you called."

"Hi Kelly, what's up?"

"Oh, I thought you may be interested in some camera footage we discovered—outside Mom's shop."

"Excellent. Were you able to determine who was responsible for the damages?"

"Well, not definitively, no. But, what was of interest is that the cameras showed Sarah hanging around outside the bakery later the same evening of the gingerbread contest."

I interrupted. "Who's Sarah?"

"Oh, remember that lady … Mom said she was fairly curt toward your friends who won the contest."

"Oh, yes. Remember her well. In fact, I swear I've seen her somewhere else since we've been here—I can't place where exactly."

"Actually, I could send you a link to view the footage yourself. That might trigger your memory. But, that's not why I texted you. The interesting part was who was with her…"

"Who?"

"Tammi! Wait, you did tell us that's the wedding you attended over the weekend, right?"

"Yeah, that's right." I looked over at Greg with a shocked look on my face. He'd already parked the car in front of our place. I signaled that I'd be along shortly; they left me sitting in the car.

Kelly was chattering about the video not being the best of quality and then I picked back up with the conversation when she said, "Looks like Tammi knows Sarah. I'm not sure how they're linked, but I'm telling you, Libby, Tammi is up to no good. Not sure that equates to being involved in your friend's death, but my instincts tell me none of this is a coincidence. The vandalism, her involvement with Sarah, or her husband's death."

A twinge coursed through my stomach; a roiling that I've felt nearly every time she mentioned Tammi's name. "I haven't had a great feeling about the woman, but really … you think she's involved? And, you think she actually *knew* Sarah—hadn't run into her on the street, asking for directions or something?"

"Well, I can't really say. But, they had quite a lengthy conversation—all caught on camera. No audio, but it went on for a while and they seemed familiar with each other." She hesitated, then continued, "I don't know, Libby. Don't you find it strange—on her wedding weekend, with tons of guests to entertain—she found her way to my mom's bakery the same night someone vandalized it? She knows the same woman who, hours prior, threw a tantrum in there … Coincidence?"

That was a good point. I needed to think through the timeline. I swore that evening after the decorating contest was when we learned Peter was missing. *Had Tammi been in town while he went on his adventure?* That was during the day, though. I thought I remembered after skiing with the rest of the group, she went home. *Or had she?* I'd have to ask around.

"Hmmm. Yeah, send me that link, I'd be interested. If nothing else, it helps with the timeline surrounding Peter's disappearance, I think." I hesitated for a moment. "Wait, you said something about leaving information for me to pick up at the bakery. Was that the camera footage?"

"Well, yes, but there was something else, too. Along with the footage, Mom was certain a small handbag that got left behind was yours, or maybe your friends."

"Oh. Huh. Not mine, but perhaps Lexi's. I'll double check with her."

Kelly's voice turned somber. "Now, with your friend's death, are you heading back to Arizona early?"

"No. We're actually going to finish our vacation. A couple of Greg's friends are wrapping up some business stuff at the deceased colleague's home. The families have all left and there isn't anything else for us to do. We'll attend the service, but we're still waiting for information about that. We'll most likely be around for the rest of the week and leave on Saturday."

"Oh, that's great. I mean, not the part of the friend dying. That's not great at all; I'm so sorry for your loss. I'm happy to hear you'll get to spend more time in our beautiful town, though."

"Yeah. It's been difficult for Greg. Hopefully, it'll get easier and we can keep him occupied. I have a feeling though, with his other friends here, he'll want to help them out however they need."

I heard a few tapping noises. "Okay, Libby … I sent you the link to view the camera footage. Let me know what you think. And hey, when you come to pick up the bag, stop in next door and say hi. You know, while you're still here, we could show you around Taos. Mom loves giving tours," she giggled. "Oh, what am I thinking? I'm sure you have your hands full. Still, if you have free time, we'd love to give you and your friends a brief tour from a local's perspective."

"That's so nice for you to offer, Kelly. Thank you.

I will chat with the group and we'll let you know. Much appreciated!"

I hopped out of the car and realized how dark and cold it'd gotten. I hurried inside and found everyone sitting around the fireplace with wine glasses in their hands.

"So cozy, you guys!" I exclaimed, as I poured myself a glass and joined them.

"What was all that about?" JJ asked me, using pinky and thumb to mimic talking on the phone.

"I guess there's footage showing Tammi and Sarah outside the bakery in the hours before the vandalism."

"Tammi? The bride?" Alexis asked.

"Yep." I nodded, and then continued to relay the rest of the conversation we'd had. In the end, I learned that Alexis also hadn't left a handbag there. We all leaned in to watch the video footage on my phone.

The footage hadn't shown vandalism, so that mystery wasn't solved. However, I had the distinct feeling this evidence led to a far deeper mystery. Related to Peter's death? I couldn't be certain.

CHAPTER SEVENTEEN

The next day, the guys skied during the morning, then joined Raj and Hector at the Schull household to help them sort through Peter's business files. Alexis, Joshua, Shadow, and I accepted the offer of the Taos tour.

Curious, Alexis and I took the bag that was found at Sweet's Sweets from Sam and tucked it away in my vehicle to examine it later. It was a bit devious to not admit it wasn't ours, but we figured it couldn't hurt to look inside. My gut feeling was that it would lead us to the grumpy woman. But, would it lead to discovering how she knew Tammi? Whatever we found, we'd return it to the rightful owner. Or the police, if it had important evidence.

We got into a bigger SUV and Kelly and Samantha showed us around the town, pointing out their favorite galleries and spots. We drove out to the Pueblo, which was beautifully covered in snow. Since it was only open for tourists seasonally, we weren't able to walk around the grounds this time of year. I snapped several photos, and we were on our way again. They took us out to the Rio Grande Gorge, which was phenomenal. Standing on an overlook, I zipped my down jacket and pulled the scarf across my face to ward off the frigid wind. We hesitated for a second to look down, but once we did, both Alexis and I exclaimed how New Mexico had its own Grand Canyon. From eight hundred feet above, we saw an impressive view of the Rio Grande River, cutting through the lava fields to form the fifty-mile-long canyon.

Kelly explained how, during the summer months, rafting is a huge draw in the area. The recent snowfall painted the black and brown hues of the lava rock with a gorgeous contrasting white. It was stunning. After several photos, with and without our new friends, we climbed back into the warmth of the vehicle and headed back toward town. They pointed out some dwellings they called Earthships— they were off-the-grid homes, literally built into the earth. Had we more time, they explained you could schedule a tour and go inside some of them. Alexis was particularly interested and mentioned maybe they'd try to arrange a tour this week before we left the area.

Back in town, Kelly kindly invited us back to her place, where she'd already prepared a steaming pot of green-chile stew and cornbread. I couldn't believe the kindness of the two ladies we'd only met days ago. As we pulled into her driveway, I was in awe of the gorgeous Victorian-styled home. With the thick snow cover and smoke billowing from the chimney, it was a picturesque scene right out of a Thomas Kinkade painting.

"Are you sure Shadow can come inside?" I hesitantly asked.

Kelly laughed. "I probably should have asked how she is around cats? We have a precocious one."

"Oh, Shadow does well with other dogs and cats. She'll be fine there." I looked around at the snow we were walking through. "She'll drag wet paws into your home, though."

She chuckled again. "Trust me, my daughter is about Joshua's age … there isn't anything worse Shadow could do. We're prepared for it."

We stepped into the mudroom and slipped off our boots and coats, also hanging our scarves on the hooks provided. Kelly handed me a small towel and I wiped down Shadow's paws really quick. As I did, the sumptuous aroma of stew hit my nostrils. We were in for a treat.

Kelly called out, "Anastasia! Scott! We're back."

From somewhere above us, we heard a screech and then footfalls bounding our way. She led us into the kitchen area, and that's where it all began. Ana plowed into the room and stopped abruptly, wide-eyed, and suddenly shy. Scott appeared behind her.

"You must be the ladies from Arizona!" he said kindly. "And this one," he knelt down to Shadow, "must be the pup who found the skunk." He then turned slightly to the right and said to Joshua, "And you must be the clever artist who designed an award-winning gingerbread house!"

Although shyly peeking over at Anastasia, Joshua's smile lit up the room. Then he quickly disappeared behind Lexi's leg again. He peeked out again at the same time the little girl did. From their mischievous expressions, I should have seen what shenanigans the afternoon would bring.

Scott shook both Alexis' and my hands, then walked

up and gave a peck on the cheeks of Samantha and Kelly.

"You're killing me, leaving us in the house all morning with these amazing smells. Let's get some food," he said, walking into the kitchen.

Already, the two five-year-olds bonded over the nine-month-old Labrador. They stood there giving Shadow pets, and she patiently let them. In fact, she was in heaven, soaking up their attention. Then, it was game on, and all three ran from the room. Our gazes collectively went toward the ceiling, hearing the stair-stomping, running, then more stairs. Suddenly, it got quiet. That's when we should have become skeptical.

Instead, Kelly and Scott graciously served up bowls of steaming stew and small plates of cornbread. Alexis and Kelly agreed the kids would seek food when hungry, until then let them be. On the table sat the butter and honey, along with place settings. We each took seats and spent the next couple of hours chatting away.

We learned Scott was an author and he also home-schooled Ana. Samantha, Scott, and Kelly told us all about the adventure of schooling their five-year-old who was beyond her years. The child had a knack for learning. They seemed to dance around the subject, but we caught several mentions, almost suggesting prescient abilities. Alexis wanted to know more.

They shared with us some possible haunted stories. It was fascinating—Lexi and I clung to their words. As the afternoon wore on, I felt a particular bond growing with the two ladies. I shared stories of unusual sensory experiences I'd had with clients during therapy sessions. It was only after Scott went back to his writing that the ladies completely opened up. It took a while—I'd caught glimpses between them throughout the meal. An unspoken 'should we tell' look crossed the table several times. Ultimately, we learned how years ago Samantha was clearing out one of the foreclosed properties and was given a dusty old box. When she handled it, it glowed warmly. When it did, she discovered an energy to it which actually gave *her* energy.

Captivated by the story, I wondered how much was true. Was she exaggerating? Then, Kelly explained, they found two more boxes over the years. One in Ireland! The stories were thought-provoking. Alexis began firing off questions for both ladies. We spent the rest of the afternoon chatting and hearing spectacular tales. From their experiences in the home we currently were in, to the local library, and more. It was enchanting—the Taos area, their stories, and how we all came together. *What's meant to be* ... I couldn't help thinking.

A loud bang sounded, bringing us back to the present. The kids, chasing Shadow, bounded down the stairs. I was glad Kelly laughed because I was becoming concerned. What were they up to? She wasn't concerned in the slightest.

Samantha got up and peeked around the corner. She smiled and signaled for Alexis to come. The two of them stretched their necks around the corner of the wall and then quickly bounced back.

"Mom!" Joshua yelled.

Lexi chuckled and then walked into the other room where the kids were; Samantha followed. Kelly and I sat sipping tea until we heard laughter erupt. We had to see what they were up to. When I walked through the doorway, I immediately cracked up. They had dressed my dog in a dress of Ana's and were now trying to get socks on her feet. No wonder Shadow had run!

Now that we had left the kitchen, Kelly offered a tour of their home. I was so grateful; I wanted to ask to see the gorgeous place, but hadn't wanted to be rude by asking. She pointed out the downstairs features, reminding us of the story about Samantha's chocolate factory. That's why Kelly's kitchen looked like a chef's dream. We headed upstairs, showing us each room.

Then we ascended the final staircase to a converted attic. We peeked in on Scott in one room, but quickly left him to concentrate on his writing. A chill took hold of me; how was he able to work in such temperatures. He hadn't appeared bothered at all. In fact, no one else mentioned being cold.

There was another door, partially opened. That's when I caught another glimpse between Samantha and Kelly … another unspoken 'should we?'. Samantha gave a slight nod, and Kelly pushed the door.

Mmmwrow!

I jolted backwards, catching the flash of black, orange, and white flash by.

Kelly giggled. "She always does that. I should have warned you. That was Eliza."

My heart calmed, realizing it was only a calico cat. The giggling stopped, and we stared at Samantha.

Her smile faded. "That's strange," she murmured.

Our eyes followed hers. There was an old book laying open. *Ancient* was more like it. The pages looked extremely delicate, something one would find in the archives of a library, only to be handled with special gloves.

Kelly's eyes widened, and she looked back toward the hallway where the cat had escaped.

"Do you think?" Sam asked her.

She shrugged. "I hope not."

Alexis and I exchanged looks and shrugged.

"Is something wrong?" I asked.

Samantha immediately placed her body between us and the book. "Nope. Nothing wrong here." Then she motioned to Kelly. "Shall we head back downstairs?"

"Yep, let's go see what those silly kids are up to," she nervously chuckled, before shepherding us back out into the hallway.

I noticed Sam delayed in following us, and after a couple of seconds, she shut the attic door behind her and locked it. I wondered what the big secret was, but decided it wasn't any of my business. Maybe it had to do with the boxes they told us about earlier? They hadn't shown us the magical boxes they mentioned earlier, which left me slightly disappointed. Again, none of our business.

By the time we found the kids, Shadow was undressed again. She looked at me pleadingly. It was then I realized why—Ana and Joshua were cutting some construction paper, making cute hats. She seemed to know what was coming. I comforted her as we all took seats in their living room. Conversation resumed, but this time more kid centric as we each received a homemade Christmas hat. Very British custom. I now saw what Scott and Kelly mentioned earlier—Ana was a creative little girl.

The afternoon sun was fading. Samantha announced she'd need to leave soon to get back to her husband and get dinner ready soon. She was our ride, so we began coaxing Joshua to help clean up and get his warm layers back on. It took a lot of persuasion. Only after we promised to work out another playdate soon did we finally get his jacket and boots on him.

CHAPTER EIGHTEEN

Greg and JJ had texted, wondering where we were, and thankfully catching us right before we headed back up the mountain. They wanted to have dinner in town; they were famished and hadn't eaten since breakfast. Alexis and I were still full of Kelly's amazing green-chile stew, but agreed to meet up with them, anyway. We decided for non-fancy, since we had Shadow and Joshua with us—and settled on the Taos Mesa Brewery. Even though it was a brewery, they were kid and dog-friendly. Both guys ordered huge gourmet burgers; Lexi and I nibbled on a shared order of nachos, which went so well with our margaritas. As a group, we'd already decided that Greg and JJ were the drivers tonight so we ladies could partake.

"So, the bakery lady invited you over to her home?" JJ questioned.

"Well, it was actually the groomer's home. Kelly, who saved Shadow from an endless skunk smell," she reminded him.

"That was so nice," Greg added.

"Yeah, it was a lovely day…"

"I made a new friend, Daddy!" Joshua shouted.

JJ smiled. "You did? Tell me all about your new friend…"

Joshua gushed about Anastasia, their cat, and all the things they did. He reached into a pocket and pulled out another paper crown. "Here daddy. For you!" he tried putting it on JJ's head, but couldn't reach. My friend, the great sport he is, got it settled into place and posed for a picture.

I noticed something fell to the floor when Joshua pulled the paper hat out. I reached down and picked it up. While they were taking photos and laughing at JJ, I unfolded what looked to be a sheet of notebook paper. On it was a beautiful pencil-etched drawing.

I tapped Alexis on her wrist, then handed over the sheet of paper. "Certainly Joshua didn't draw this, right?" I asked, wondering if my godson was some artistic savant.

Her face contorted, questioning where I'd found it.

"It fell out of Joshua's pocket when he gave JJ that hat."

"Wow. No, there's no way this is something he drew. This is professional."

Both of us realized this meant he must have taken something from Kelly's home.

Lexi interrupted the conversation he was having with JJ. "Hey, sweetie … where'd you get this?"

Joshua's eyes lit up. "Ana made that for me!" He

grabbed to get the paper back from his mom. She held her hand up higher, just out of his reach.

"Well, let me see it ... hold on." She examined the piece. "This is *really good*. You said Ana drew it? You saw her draw it?"

"Yes! Upstairs in that little room where the cat lives." He squirmed in his seat, still trying to get at it.

Lexi looked skeptically over at me.

I asked Joshua, "Can I see it?"

He nodded, excited.

I took the page from Lexi and looked closer at the drawing. Struck by how intricately detailed it was, I glanced up at Lexi again. We both exchanged incredulous looks. *How could a five-year-old create something like this?*

The illustration was separated into three scenes, but strangely appeared to meld into one, seamlessly. There was a mountain with what I presumed to be ski runs, including tiny skiers. At the base of the mountain, there was a small town, and in the distance, I could make out a large canyon. Ah, it had to be a drawing of Taos. Within that scene, there were businesses in the town—*oh look, a bakery*. The child was clearly proud of her grandmother's work. The detail was amazing. I looked closer then and saw she'd drawn women standing in front of the bakery. This Ana was far more talented than I'd given credit for, if she had truly drawn the picture. Then I remembered her parents had mentioned something about her special gifts. My eye caught something else—written in tiny script near the skiers was **'memujidupe'**. My heart skipped a beat. I'd seen that only recently. *Where had I seen it? What does it mean?*

Suddenly, I remembered the piece of paper I'd shoved into my pocket from Peter's nightstand. I gasped. It was the same word!

Alexis questioned, "What is it?"

"Do you see that?" I pointed to the letters.

She squinted, then pulled her glasses from her purse. "Memu … what?"

"Exactly. I found that word—or whatever it is—when I was at Peter's house snooping around."

She gave me the side-eye; I presumed it was about the snooping part.

"No, really … that's not even a proper word. What are the chances I've seen it in two different locations over the past twenty-four hours?"

"Maybe it's a regional cultural term? We should ask Sam or Kelly. They're very knowledgeable."

I nodded, continuing to stare at the drawing, absolutely mesmerized by the variety of things I kept noticing. I noticed that Ana had drawn one woman as a blonde and the other had dark hair. Leaning in closer, I could see the lady with the lighter hair also had on a skiing outfit. *Was I making this up, or was her outfit bejeweled? Nah.* But, what were the odds of a child we'd recently met drawing the likeness of a person I'd recognize? A chill ran through me—a chill eerily similar to the one earlier in the attic.

Joshua bounced in his chair, eager for me to hand the drawing over to him.

"Alexis—do these two women look similar to those in that video we saw?"

She finished her sip of margarita, then squinted to see the paper. "It's probably a stretch, but I see where you may have gotten that idea." She handed it across the table to JJ, who was also now curious.

JJ looked at it, then at me. "Joshua's new friend drew

this?" He scrutinized for a moment, then handed it over to his son, two seconds away from a complete meltdown. "That's incredibly talented."

"But, did you really look at it?" I asked with impatience. "All the details—the whole Taos Valley, including the bakery?"

"Oh wow! You got all of that from a drawing of some mountain town?" he laughed. "I mean, it's *good*, but really? I think your tour and Taos experience might be influencing your perception, maybe."

Alexis and JJ broke out laughing. Greg was eager to see what we were talking about, but was too nervous to ask Joshua for it.

I sweetly asked the boy, "Hey, honey … Auntie Libby would really like to show Greg that special picture Ana drew. Can we see it for a couple more minutes? Please?"

He looked down at the paper in his hands, then his little eyes looked up at us. "Okay, but only a little." He cautiously handed it back to me.

I leaned over to Greg and pointed out the features I had described to the others. He nodded, then agreed with JJ. I smacked his arm. "C'mon! Do you see those letters there?"

He nodded after dramatically squinting to detect them.

"When I was in Peter's room, snoop … well, *looking around*, I found that same word written on a note in his nightstand drawer. Isn't that strange?"

He read it again and agreed. "It has no meaning I'm aware of."

"It has to be a clue! A *code*…" I exclaimed. "Earlier, I assumed it was some acronym used in Peter's business. Didn't think much of it. But, now … what are the chances a *child used the same word* in her own illustration? That's weird, right?"

"Ana's not weird!" Joshua yelled.

"No, no, sweetie. She's not. We're talking about this word." I pointed it out to him as I handed the paper back. He stared blankly.

"She copied this from a book," he muttered softly. "Fast!" He made a zoom motion with his hands and sounds like he was racing cars around the table.

Lexi and I stared at him, then at each other. *What did that mean?*

Clearly, we had to discuss this with Samantha. That would have to wait until tomorrow.

CHAPTER NINETEEN

The shrill of the phone ringing broke through my dreams. I startled, sitting upright. Greg snored loudly and with no indication he'd heard the phone. Again, the music of a raucous disco sounded from his bedstand. I stood up and walked around the bed to find the source.

Faint light cast into the room from a skylight. The clock read shortly before seven o'clock. I pressed the side button on the phone to silence it; the display read 'My Man Raj.' I pressed the answer button and walked outside the bedroom.

"Hi Raj, it's Libby," I whispered.

"Oh jeez, I'm so sorry to have awakened you!"

"It's okay, what's up?"

"I wanted to see if Greg would come with me to Santa

Fe this morning—you're more than welcome, too. Last night, we finally located the helicopter pilot who took Peter backcountry skiing."

"Oooh, that's great. I'll wake him up. Hey, why Santa Fe? It wasn't a locally operated adventure?"

"Nope. The company's headquarters are in Santa Fe. Guess the pilot himself was someone Peter had known for a while—through his business dealings. I don't know. I'm hoping to learn more in person."

"Okay, give me ten minutes. I'll have Greg call you." I hung up, then shook Greg awake.

Once we explained to Lexi and JJ about the impromptu trip to Santa Fe, they decided they'd rather ski today. Time here in New Mexico was running out.

"Oh, are you going to call Sam and let her know about that drawing Joshua came home with?"

Lexi nodded. "After skiing, later this afternoon, I'll call her. You know, I spent more time looking at it after Joshua went to bed. It really is intricate with details, isn't it?"

I chuckled. It seemed unbelievable. There *had* to be another explanation. A five-year-old could not have drawn that.

"Okay, we're off. This shouldn't take too long, I wouldn't think. Couple of hours driving and maybe an hour talking with the pilot. We might even be back by lunchtime. I'll text you," I said, giving Lexi a hug goodbye.

The drive was uneventful. Raj drove us in a comfortable Escalade. Shadow and I rode in the back seat, and Greg helped to navigate. Exactly one hour later, we pulled up at a hangar at the small airport. A short man I'd describe as being in his late fifties walked from the helicopter toward us. He was dressed in a blue flight suit, wore dark aviator sunglasses, and had a closely cropped full head of salt and pepper hair. Raj introduced us to William Davila, and as I shook his hand, I couldn't help but think that he looked like the quintessential pilot. He asked us to call him Will.

With a quick show of his hand, he bent over to pet Shadow. He turned, and we followed him inside the large metal building.

"I'm not sure what I could tell you that I haven't already told the police," he began. "Peter Schull hired our company to take them to an established backcountry ski area. We did that. The whole deal was that I drop skiers off—the rest of the journey was up to them to get back to the resort area. Conditions were great that day ... well, until late during the night, that is. From what Peter told me, they were both experienced skiers."

I interrupted. "You keep saying 'they' ... someone else was with Peter?"

Raj and Greg had picked up on that too; we all eagerly waited for his response.

Will's eyes met each one of ours with a look of confusion. "Of course, someone was with him. We would never agree to take a lone skier to the back country—that's not safe."

Greg softly asked, "What was the other passenger's name?"

"Oh, for heaven's sake, I've given all this information to the police! Our company did nothing wrong here." Clearly agitated, Will picked up a rag lying nearby and anxiously started wiping down his aircraft.

Raj stepped forward. "Please. Peter was my business partner and a dear friend of ours. We aren't accusing *you* of anything. We simply hadn't been told anyone was with him that day … but that information actually makes me feel a bit better. I couldn't imagine Peter going alone, and now we have someone else who may know what happened. What was the passenger's name? Do you know where we could find him?"

All eyes were on Will when he turned around to face us. He nervously paced. "This is an ongoing investigation. I'm not comfortable sharing anymore. The police…"

"Please … who was the guy with him?" I pleaded.

He stopped and slowly turned around. "I don't know. Long blonde hair. Had a beanie, goggles, and complete snow gear on the entire time. I wouldn't be able to identify the person even if they found 'em," he quietly said, bowing his head. "Look, I've lost all credibility already. I really don't know how much more I can tell you."

Greg asked, "Who have you lost credibility with?"

"The police, for one. But, most importantly, my employer; the management at High Country Tours. This is why they've grounded me. You see, there's only record of one passenger: Peter Schull. When I tried telling them he unexpectedly brought someone with him that day … well, let's just say I'm in trouble for doing a favor for my friend." He kicked at the ground, frustrated.

"I've been grounded until the investigation clears the company of any wrongdoing. That's per my management. The police have already said they ruled his death an accident. I think skiing accident … exposure to the elements, I'm not sure? I swear—we did *nothing* wrong here. My job was simply to take a client to the area, leave them, and return. We're not responsible if they can't make it back. All of this is bullshit!"

"Understandable—we believe you." I reached out,

trying to comfort. "I'm sure the company has signed paperwork acknowledging that they can't hold you responsible, right?"

Will's face lightened up. "Oh yes! Ironclad contract that protects us from lawsuits." His face drooped again. "Except I failed to get the other passenger's paperwork in order. Peter was in a hurry … I allowed myself to be pushed into bending the rules for a friend. That'll be my last mistake."

"Oh. And no one has come forward?"

"No. I tried telling them there was another person. But, since I hadn't completed the paperwork, I can't prove that. If only I hadn't let her onboard."

"Wait. You said 'her' … it was a woman?" I questioned.

"Honestly, these days you can't be sure. I guess I assumed that because of the thin physique and long blonde hair."

Greg asked, "You'd know by their voice, wouldn't you?"

"Never spoke."

"Mannerisms? Like, how they walk or sit?" I added.

"Lady, I was busy. I didn't pay any attention to that stuff."

I looked around the hangar for cameras. "Certainly, the two were captured on security footage, right?"

He shook his head. "No, not here. I picked them up at the Taos airport. They never came to this hangar. That's why when I got there, and didn't have paperwork with me for an additional passenger, I protested against an extra person. Peter started pulling out bills—*large ones*." Will looked embarrassed. "He paid handsomely. I had enough fuel, so I bent the rules."

"I'm sure the Taos airport has some footage of the three of you, right?"

He shook his head. "I don't know, but they haven't provided anything yet, or my story would already be validated."

Interesting.

A thought occurred to me. "Any chance we could see in the helicopter? I've always wanted to ride inside one and I don't see police crime scene tape around. Would that be okay?"

The pilot got excited to show off his ship. As we climbed aboard the white and blue machine, I heard him mention it was a Bell 206 JetRanger III, same as used by news agencies, police, and various tour operators. The pilot took his time explaining what all the controls do; Greg and Raj were captivated. Shadow and I sat in one of the two back row passenger seats; she was at my feet. I heard her nose sniffing around, and when I became bored with the pilot-speak, I also began doing my own sniffing around; not literally. *What exactly was I looking for?* I wasn't sure; maybe an identification card, something that said who this person was with Peter. Silly me—like anything was that easy. And as if the police hadn't thoroughly searched the helicopter for evidence. *Was the extra passenger a woman?* That was an interesting tidbit the pilot shared—also could explain why Tammi wasn't aware of Peter's excursion.

"Hey, Will …" I called out. He finished his sentence about rotors, then looked back at me. "The police have searched the aircraft, right?"

He shook his head. "Why?"

"Oh, well, you said they grounded it until the investigation was over."

"Right. The bosses made that decision because of my breaking the company's protocol. They're punishing me. The police interviewed me and my boss, but that was it. They weren't concerned with the actual helicopter."

Interesting.

"And they aren't worried another person is potentially missing … or dead?"

He only shrugged

A chill ran up my spine. Shadow diverted my attention when I saw half her body was under the seat.

"Shadow, c'mon …" I knelt down to grab for her harness when I couldn't budge her with the leash. Grunting, I got my head down where I could see better. "Get out of there. Want a cookie?" I coaxed.

She began backing out, and I moved out of her way. When she stood, I saw she was covered in dust bunnies. I reached into my pocket and grabbed a cookie—she snatched it up, so proud of herself. I started to brush the dust off, when I saw what looked like blonde hair strands. Turning my head toward the cockpit, it was obvious they were busy talking helicopters again. I reached back into my other jacket pocket and found a clean tissue. Carefully, I used the tissue to grab the hair from Shadow's back and then wrapped it up tightly. *Could this possibly lead us to the person Peter was with?* Who knows, but I figured it couldn't hurt, and hopefully JJ could help get it analyzed.

On the way back to Taos, Greg looked back at me. "You did what?"

"*Shadow* dug around under the back passenger seat. When I finally got her out, I found this." I held up the wadded-up tissue, and carefully displayed my treasure to him. "Maybe this hair will lead us to who was with Peter that day?"

Raj chuckled. "Good going, Shadow."

Greg turned to his friend. "Is it only me, or do you also find it odd the police don't seem like they're being thorough?"

Raj shrugged. "I don't know about that. If you're asking about searching the helicopter—maybe. But, if they're investigating an accident, the helicopter wasn't part of that." He considered for a second. "Peter with another woman? Do you really think that's true?"

"Can't imagine," Greg said, shaking his head.

I sat in the back listening to them banter back and forth. My mind drifted, remembering that I had seen Tammi skiing with someone else—maybe that was their deal? Maybe their relationship was open. I'd heard of that type of thing, although for the life of me, I couldn't figure out how it'd work out.

The drive back to Taos was relatively quick. I had texted JJ and Alexis; they were done skiing for the day and we all agreed to meet in town for lunch. We tried another recommended place—the Taoseño, which was supposed to have the most authentic New Mexican food in the area. They weren't wrong; it was delicious.

"I brought that drawing, oh and the purse, to return to Samantha, if we can just drop by the bakery when we're done," Lexi said to the table.

The guys were distracted, but I'd completely forgotten about that purse we picked up from Sweet's Sweets yesterday.

"Wasn't Sarah's?" I asked. Lexi knew I was talking

about the purse that Sam had discovered at the bakery after the contest.

"There was no identification in it at all—I do not know whose it was. As you and I discussed, though, I'll explain it was my mistake. I mean, it looks somewhat similar to that one I have back home, right?" She blushed, feeling embarrassed that they deceived Sam. "Well, anyway, she can check with her regular customers after we return it."

That reminded me of what was in my pocket. "Hey JJ, do you have any contacts here in Taos? With the police department…?"

He shook his head. "Why?"

I pulled out the tissue, carefully opened a corner, proudly showing it to him. "I have some hair I'd like analyzed."

"Jesus, Libby! Whose hair have you stolen?"

Offended, I scoffed. "I didn't *steal* anything, JJ." I explained how I came into possession of the blonde hairs and why I thought they could be important. "Can I walk into the police station and ask for them to be examined?"

He laughed. "No, Libby. It doesn't work like that."

Before getting brushed off, I turned to Alexis. "Didn't Samantha say her husband was the former Taos Sheriff?"

She nodded. JJ's eyebrows rose; his head moving left and right, looking at both of us perplexed. "No, Libby. Please don't."

I shoved the tissue back into my pocket. Somehow, I would find a way.

CHAPTER TWENTY

Sweet's Sweets had a gaggle of ladies crowded around the bakery cabinet, picking out their confections. A pleasant woman we hadn't met before was at the counter, patiently helping them. Her name badge read: Jen.

The ladies paid for their purchases and skirted around us to leave. Alexis and I stepped up to the counter.

"How may I help you today?" Jen asked.

"We're looking for Samantha. Is she in today?" I inquired.

"I'm sorry, she isn't expected in today. Is there something I can help you with?"

Lexi and I shared a glance. Then she explained, "Um, no. We were with her and Kelly yesterday, and I think my son may have taken something that wasn't his." She patted the top of Joshua's head. "We need to return it."

Joshua pouted, saying quietly, "She made it for me. She wanted me to have it."

"Oh! Kelly is working next door ... maybe she can help?"

"Of course. We should have started there since it was her home he took it from. Silly us. Thank you for your help."

"No problem. Need a pastry or muffin before you go?" she smiled.

We explained we already had a week's supply back at our rental—plus that amazing cake we'd yet to cut into.

"Oh! You were the winners of the gingerbread contest! Okay ... congratulations!" Jen exclaimed.

I pointed to Alexis and Joshua. The boy smiled widely at the friendly young woman.

"Thank you again," I started, and we turned to head out the door. "Oh! You got the window fixed, I see ..." I hadn't noticed when we walked in, but now there was a new winter scene made from cakes, cookies, and beautifully decorated slices.

"Yes, thankfully. It was so cold in here for several days."

Joshua pulled at Lexi's jeans. "Mom, are they going to put our house in the window again?"

"Oh honey, I'm afraid not. Someone stole it, unfortunately."

Joshua pouted on the way out, and we thanked Jen again for her time.

We popped on over to the groomer's shop, leaving the guys chatting outside in front of our vehicles. Once the chime sounded, the swinging doors that separated the grooming area opened. Anastasia came running out when she saw it was Joshua. The two hugged and disappeared through the swinging doors before Lexi could say anything.

Kelly walked out with gloved hands and water dripping down the apron she was wearing. "Hey! Give me a couple minutes … I'm nearly ready to hand this one off to my colleague."

"Is Joshua okay being back there?" Lexi asked nervously.

"Oh, yes … will help keep Ana out of my hair, honestly," Kelly chuckled. "Be right back."

A couple minutes later, Samantha walked in the front door.

"Hello! Surprised to see you two," she greeted warmly, giving us both hugs. "Shadow didn't play with another skunk, did she?"

"No, no. We're only waiting for Kelly to finish up," I stated.

Lexi's mocha complexion flushed with embarrassment. "Sam, I think Joshua took something he shouldn't have yesterday … from Kelly's home." She reached into her purse and pulled out the folded-up paper.

Samantha leaned in as she unfolded it. The gasp took us by surprise; Lexi looked as though she wanted to disappear. By Sam's reaction, it was obvious it was something the young child shouldn't have had in his possession.

Lexi tried to explain, "He said Ana drew it for him. That it was a gift. Clearly, that can't be…"

Samantha's face went white. "Ana drew this?"

Kelly came through the doors. "Sorry … oh, hi Mom! You're early." She stopped in her tracks when she saw what Samantha was holding in her hands. "Where did you get that?"

Samantha looked at Lexi and me. Kelly stepped up,

took the paper from her mother, and stared at it.

Awkwardly, I tried again to explain. "Joshua said Ana drew this for him."

Kelly carefully handed the drawing back to Sam, then turned to us. "Thank you for bringing this to us." She and Samantha again shared a look between them that I took to mean, 'should we tell them?'.

"Is there something more … I mean, we're *truly sorry* if Joshua took something he shouldn't have," I rambled, trying to find an appropriate apology.

After a second of uncomfortable silence, Samantha answered. "No. Joshua didn't do anything wrong. If Ana made this for him, then it's rightfully his." She looked down at the paper again, mesmerized by it.

"Then …" I wasn't sure how to communicate my concern.

Kelly shared, "We've known for some time that Ana is special … wise beyond her years. But, this…" Samantha and Kelly both stood shaking their heads, eyeing the details in the picture.

Lexi agreed. "It *is* a genuine work of art. Amazing what your daughter has come up with."

The ladies found no words, but kept shaking their heads. Finally, Kelly changed subjects.

"Mom, you're early. Are you sure you want her *all* afternoon?"

"Of course," Sam gushed. Aware we were still in the room, she explained. "Beau, uh, my husband, has been exercising our horses using a sleigh this winter. Today, we're going to take Ana on a ride and to give Kelly a bit of a break." She looked toward the back room where she heard the little kid squeals, then whispered, "We've got some surprises in store. Hey, would Joshua like to join us—she'd *love* that! She hasn't stopped talking about him since you left yesterday."

"I'm sure he'd love it. But, uh…" Lexi looked at me before continuing. "We hadn't really talked about our afternoon/evening plans yet, have we?" She turned back toward Sam. "I'd need to talk to my husband first."

"Sure, sure. Our ranch isn't located too far from where you're staying, if that's what you are concerned about?"

The kids came flying through the door. "Mom! Guess what the little dog did?" Joshua screeched, pointing behind him. "He shook water *everywhere!*" Both he and Ana squealed with delight and then ran back into the grooming room.

Kelly decided she needed to supervise and followed them.

Lexi asked Sam, "Are you absolutely sure you're up for two of them?"

Sam laughed. "Oh, we'd love to have their energy around. What fun!"

Lexi and I popped outside to find the guys; she and JJ decided Joshua would have a ball on the sleigh ride. In the meantime, Samantha had called home to consult with her husband. She and Beau invited everyone out to their ranch for dinner after the kids' sleigh ride. He had brisket in the smoker and looked forward to meeting Sam's new friends. We left Joshua with Samantha and Kelly and headed back to the ski valley.

By four o'clock that afternoon, we pulled up to their beautiful ranch. Fields layered in crystalized, sparkling snow glittered as we looked out across toward the tree line for the sleigh. Kelly came out the front door of the two-story log home and greeted us.

"They should come from that direction any time now," she said. "I texted with Mom and she said the kids were having so much fun."

Alexis and JJ appeared relieved to hear that. Greg pointed in the distance. Shadow barked. There they were—looking like a scene from a Hallmark Christmas movie. Alexis pulled her phone out and started shooting video. Ana and Joshua waved wildly once they were closer and discovered they were being filmed. They were bundled up and adorable. I zipped up my jacket and pulled my gloves from their pockets. The temperature plummeted as soon as the sun had gone behind the mountain.

Beau expertly maneuvered the horses over to their expansive barn, and their dogs followed obediently off-leash. Shadow was beside herself with excitement; she pulled hard at the leash, eager to go meet the kids and some new four-legged friends. As the sleigh slowed to a stop outside the barn doors, I saw there were a couple of ranch hands coming to help Beau.

"Come, let's get some drinks while we wait for them to come inside," Kelly said.

"I'm going to go supervise the dog's greetings. If I don't get her over there, she's going to make me her sleigh soon." As soon as I gave an inch, Shadow was already launching herself toward the barn.

"Very good. We'll be waiting inside," she called out as we hurried away. She led my friends through the large wooden front entryway.

As we approached, Beau gave their dogs a command,

and they both obediently sat. I stopped and made Shadow sit as well. It worked for a second, but for a nine-month-old pup, her hind-end kept popping up off the ground and I gently encouraged her to sit again. Beau helped me introduce each dog individually —Ranger was also a black Lab, and Nellie, a gorgeous border collie. After they'd all sniffed one another, and everything appeared to go well, we allowed them some space to play. Shadow was far more energetic than Beau's older dogs. Regardless, in no time at all, they accepted her into their pack.

Not long after, we joined the others in the house. As Beau, Sam, the kids, and I took off our coats and boots, I smelled that brisket they'd mentioned earlier. Kelly's husband, Scott, was inside, casually watching some game on TV with JJ and Greg. Kelly and Alexis were in the kitchen and had opened a bottle of Merlot. Samantha had gone upstairs to change her clothes. Beau grabbed a beer from the fridge and joined the guys in the living room.

"This is quite some place; I love it!" I told Kelly

"Yeah, it's been great for Ana to have her grandparents close by. There are lots of life lessons to be learned on a ranch too," she chuckled.

My nose caught the scent of dinner again. "Wow, smells amazing in here."

"Oh, you are in for a treat. Beau's smoked brisket is legendary around here," Scott called out, overhearing my remark.

The kids were beyond excited. Each of them was trying to be the first one to tell us all about their afternoon. Scott muted the TV to listen, and I sat back and watched it all unfold as their parents tried to keep up with the story.

Samantha and Beau made putting an impromptu

dinner gathering of ten look so easy. After spending all afternoon with two exuberant five-year-olds, I was in awe. I couldn't have done it. They called everyone to the table, and we devoured brisket, green-chile macaroni and cheese, salad, and homemade focaccia bread.

After eating, Greg and I helped to load the dishwater. Sam tried to protest, but it was the least we could do after their graciousness. Beau and JJ made fast friends, chatting about their collective law enforcement experiences. Even though retired, Beau still spoke of his time on the force as though he were still there.

I was nearly done wiping down countertops when I remembered that tissue in my jacket. Greg had already joined Scott in front of the TV. Both were cheering on their team. Looking over at JJ and Beau, I saw they were deep in conversation about a recent case in the Phoenix area.

I walked back to the front entryway and found my jacket on the hook. I prayed it hadn't fallen out somewhere along the way. When I reached into my jacket pocket, I found the hair pieces still bundled.

JJ passed by me in the hallway on his way to the bathroom. I found Beau still seated at the table next to Samantha.

"Hey, Beau." I wormed my way into the seat that JJ vacated. "I heard the two of you talking about your time in office as Sheriff. Sounds like you might still have some good contacts in town?"

Samantha laughed. "Beau knows everyone in town."

I pulled out my tissue, gaining an interested expression from the former Sheriff. "I'm not sure if Samantha or JJ has told you about Greg's friend who went missing? And, uh, well, he's been found deceased this week."

"Yeah, Sam told me. I've actually heard rumblings around town about that, too. Guess I didn't realize until tonight how well you knew him. Seems the police might believe it was an accidental death?"

Greg heard we were talking about Peter. He abandoned the TV again, standing behind me with his hands on my shoulders, and joined our conversation. "There are a few things that don't make sense though. Several of us who have known Peter for a long time think there's more to the story."

"Oh, I see." Beau got up and fetched another beer from the cooler. "What's your theory?" he questioned Greg and me as he retook his seat.

"Well, for instance, we only learned today that there was someone else with Peter on the backcountry ski trip."

"Certainly, the police are following that lead," he stated.

"We're not so sure. The pilot's failure to follow procedure may have complicated matters." Greg took a sip of his beer, then set it on the table next to me.

"While we were onboard the helicopter, Shadow found this." I pulled the tissue out and carefully displayed the contents.

"What's that?" Beau asked, pointing at the tissue.

"Blonde hairs she found nosing under the passenger seat earlier. Yeah, it's hard to see them in this white tissue."

Samantha got up and rifled through the kitchen drawer.

Beau leaned in a little closer, then sat back. "What's your angle?"

Samantha handed me a plastic baggie. "Here, throw that in there."

JJ walked back into the room at the same time. I saw

his eyes roll before he sat down in the chair next to me. "Libby, you're not pestering our new friend here with that, are you?"

I gave a sheepish grin, then answered Beau's question. "The pilot told us that the extra passenger had long, blonde hair. Perhaps these belong to that person? Do you know someone who could discreetly help us?"

Beau cleared his throat. "Normally, I'd say the department is too busy to bother. Plus, isn't it evidence— why discreetly?" he questioned suspiciously.

"Well, uh … I mean, we don't really *know* for sure it's evidence. The police don't seem to be interested in the pilot or the aircraft. Before getting anyone in further trouble, when it could be nothing, I thought maybe…"

He chuckled and leaned forward, taking the baggie from me, turning it over, and scrutinizing it. He looked up at me again. "I just had breakfast with one of my buddies yesterday morning. Let me see what I can do," he said, smiling at both Samantha and me. "No promises. And, if there is a match in the system—this gets turned over as evidence."

"Thank you!" I gushed.

JJ also looked pleased. Another lawman who took his job seriously.

Kelly, who was in the living room with Scott and the kids, called out, "Hey, guys, stop talking shop and come see what Scott put together."

We turned their way and saw a slideshow starting on their large TV. It was the sleigh ride adventure. Joshua and Ana looked cute in photos of snowball fights, roasting marshmallows, and riding in the sleigh.

I glanced questioningly at Lexi. She shrugged, then

whispered, "I sent our photos to Kelly before dinner."

Samantha came over to us. "Thank you for allowing Joshua to join us today. That was so special for Ana—actually, I think for both of them."

Lexi agreed. "No, thank *you* for inviting him. This experience," she said, pointing toward the TV, "is far richer than sitting in front of video games at home."

Kelly joined the rest of us standing behind the sofa and gave a slight nod to Samantha. The slideshow had finished, and the guys had moved along to talking all things 'ranch'. The ladies quietly maneuvered Lexi and me down a hallway and into another sitting room. They closed the door to this room, and their secretiveness caused us to exchange worried glances.

"Is something wrong?" I asked.

Kelly hesitated, looking at Sam. I caught the slight nod from her mother. "Listen, Libby … Alexis. We need to fill you in on something."

I saw Samantha move away, toward a sideboard, opening its center drawer. She pulled out a piece of paper, and as she came closer again, I realized it was Ana's drawing we'd handed over to her earlier. Clearing her throat, she laid it out fully on the coffee table in front of us. Kelly turned up the lighting in the room.

"Remember yesterday at my house … we were upstairs, where the cat ran out?"

We both nodded.

"Well, along with those boxes we've told you about," Kelly hesitated, looking at her mom for help. "We, uh…"

"We came upon an ancient book not long ago," Sam finished Kelly's sentence.

I remembered the book with the fragile-looking pages.

Both Lexi and I were riveted to their words.

Sam continued, "Now, we're not completely sure, but in the past, this book has helped us with some local mysteries we found ourselves involved in. We're still learning, but it appears to be some sort of spell book..."

Sam gave the go ahead with a nod; Kelly pointed to the drawing. "We suspect this drawing has something to do with your friend's disappearance."

My jaw dropped. "How?"

They both started pointing out features on the paper. Details that earlier seemed insignificant. Now, all of us began theorizing, discussing the finer points of the illustration.

Sam continued. "Once you left, Kelly and I returned to the room where we had seen our book displayed earlier. We have always safely tucked it away in that room, away from the rest of the family—it's hard to explain. Seeing it out in the open came as a shock to us. We think Joshua and Ana may have been playing in there."

Lexi immediately spoke up. "I'm so sorry if they..."

"No, no. It's okay. They didn't hurt anything," Kelly countered.

Sam and Kelly smiled at one another and then Sam explained. "Joshua said Ana drew this, right?" We nodded. "Yes. She did, and we honestly don't understand *how*, but we suspect that there is a connection with that ancient document. Between her, the boxes, Eliza, and who knows what other magic, it somehow conveys messages to us. We *think* it may be communicating something about Peter's death."

Lexi and I stared at each other, confused. "Eliza?"

Sam reminded us about the cat.

Kelly appeared to understand our reactions. "Yeah, we don't know either."

Sam shrugged. "The only thing I can think of is that we—our family—" she pointed her fingers back and forth between Kelly and herself, then us. "We're somehow connected to you."

Speechless, they both pointed back to the drawing. Besides the ski hill, a helicopter in the sky, and two little skiers off in the wide-open valley, they drew our attention to the town's scene. The bakery! I felt a chill crawl over my skin.

How? Were these two incidents connected somehow?

CHAPTER TWENTY-ONE

Greg's phone chimed on our way home a little while later. I picked it up and read the text message while he drove.

Service has been scheduled. Saturday 10:30 a.m. in ABQ.

Silence enveloped our vehicle for the rest of the way.

Alexis and JJ beat us home after we'd stopped for gas. By the time we walked inside, they were busy getting Joshua bathed and ready for bed. I started the tea kettle and changed into my comfy fleece pants and sweatshirt. Greg built a fire, and we sat quietly staring at the flames.

After several minutes, I asked softly, "I guess we'll stay on another day in Albuquerque and head home on Sunday now?"

Greg contemplated, then nodded slowly. "Man, I still

can't believe that Peter is gone. The news about his service has made it seem real now, I guess."

We sat quietly. I reflected on our time in New Mexico. It was Thursday night—the week had gone by so fast. But, not necessarily all in a good way. We'd planned to do a lot more skiing, for one. A pang of guilt hit me, realizing skiing should be the last thing I was concerned about.

Eventually, Alexis and JJ joined us.

Lexi brought in some chamomile tea, handing me one of the steaming hot mugs. She sat next to me when Greg moved to tend the fire. "I can't stop thinking about what Sam and Kelly divulged," she mentioned. We turned, sitting cross-legged, facing each other on the cushy sofa.

"I know!" I'd been excited to discuss it with her ever since we left Samantha's, but with the news of the service dampening the mood, I dropped it.

Greg and JJ now sat, their heads tilted, showing interest. They moved in closer and we shared a little of what we learned about the spell book and a possible connection to the drawing. While we took turns explaining, they nodded politely and listened. Once we were done, they looked at each other, laughed, then dismissed it as a bunch of woo-woo. They moved away again, closer to the fireplace, and onto the subject about how cool Beau's ranch was.

Lexi pulled out her phone. She'd taken a picture of the drawing unbeknownst to me. Thankfully, because I had forgotten some elements, I took the phone and studied the picture. I zoomed in on various aspects; something seemed different but I couldn't tell exactly. We chatted away, sharing theories.

Then, confused as ever, I closed my eyes, wondering what it all meant. *How could some ancient book predict hundreds (or thousands) of years later what our current situation would be? Did I really believe in this? And, even if I did, what exactly was it telling us?* Sam and Kelly seemed to have faith. I couldn't wrap my head around it fully, but there was something tapping at the edges of my brain. My subconscious telling me to pay attention? I couldn't be sure.

Lexi tapped my knee, and I opened my eyes again. "Can I see it again?" she asked.

I handed it over.

We both shook our heads in wonder.

"I suppose time will tell?" she said. "There are many cultures that rely heavily on ancient writings and folklore. Signs. Intuition. I suppose this isn't much different?"

I shrugged. It was so hard to know how it all fit in. "But, the words in that book are gibberish; how do we know the translation?"

"Exactly. Strange how they believe the boxes, the *cat*, and Ana have assisted with mysteries in the past."

"Yeah, that's bizarre—And is that what Ana did this time? Translated events through illustrations? We're supposed to believe she's connected somehow; that she picks things up from ancient writings. A five-year-old girl? Really?" I lifted my hands, moving my fingers about. "All soooo *spooky...*" I teased.

Lexi giggled, and the guys looked over, rolling their eyes at us.

I changed subjects. "In other news, they have set the service date and time. Two days from now."

Lexi reached out and patted my knee. "Oh. I'm so sorry all this has happened. I feel for Peter's family. Greg. Ugh, how awful. And, not to mention, what a way to end a vacation, huh?"

"I suppose you guys will want to beeline it home on Saturday, as was planned originally?" I asked her.

"I'll discuss it with JJ, but yes, I assume that's what we'll do."

Several more hours vanished as we sat around talking. The guys decided they'd check in with Hector and Raj in the morning. Other than that, we didn't have much of a plan for our final day of vacation together.

* * *

Light filled the suite. Had I known then that I should have rolled over, closed my eyes, and gone back to sleep, maybe I could have saved myself from an entire day of chaos. Instead, I rolled over, reached across the covers, and discovered Greg wasn't there.

Relaxing back on my pillow, my brain started a replay of everything that had transpired over the past week. The parties, the skiing, but then the worry when Peter went missing, and of course, the sadness when we learned he'd passed. I smiled, thinking of the new friends we'd met in Taos … as well as Greg's family members I'd met. It was a lot to experience the duality of witnessing new love and friendships, and also enduring tragic loss and emotional upheaval.

My phone rang. When I lifted it, I saw it was Samantha Sweet so I punched the button.

"Hi Sam," I answered.

I heard a sharp inhale. "Oh, no. Did I wake you?"

"No, no. Lazy morning, but I'm awake."

"Oh good. I've learned some new information," she started, and quickly launched into a story about Kelly and some old photos. For so early in the morning, the lady sure was energetic. "You see, they were from the time that she and Tammi worked together, years back. Last night when she got home, she found them." She paused, sucking in a large breath and then pressed on. "You will never believe what she's discovered!"

My brain finally caught up. "What?"

"Tammi's aunt … that she lived with here in Taos. You'll never believe who she is?"

"Who?"

"Sarah!"

"Who is Sarah?"

"The lady who was at the gingerbread baking contest. The one who left all upset when Joshua won."

"Oh yeah. And?"

"Well, don't you find it interesting how they are related? I don't believe it could be coincidence."

"Ohhh. I see what you're getting at. Or, is it that …"

She excitedly talked over me. "Libby—we went back and viewed the security footage; from the vandalism. Kelly and I both *swear* the dark-haired lady was Sarah. Yeah, I know, the video is grainy and not the best, but you'd have to see it."

"Ohhh…"

"AND, if you compare screenshots with the illustration Ana did … you know, while handling our book. They are *identical*. I believe we're on to something."

"Whoa…" I muttered. If what Sam was saying was true, it explained why the lady looked familiar to me. She must have been at those wedding parties. "Have you located her? Told the police about her?"

"Yes, I dialed you the second we got off the phone

with the police."

"Wow, Sam … I'm relieved to know you possibly found the person responsible for the damages to your bakery. That's fantastic."

There was a slight pause. Then she clarified. "Libby— it's not only about my bakery. Remember us telling you about how we've solved several local crimes, and we're confident the book assisted us?"

"Yeah, I remember."

"Kelly and I believe that it's leading us to helping you with the truth about Peter's death."

My heart leaped. "Are you serious?"

She continued, explaining each element in the illustration and why they could be important to Peter's situation. "We really need to get together again. Can you and Lexi come by this afternoon?"

My voice dropped. "Oh. Uh, I don't know, Sam. Peter's service is in Albuquerque tomorrow morning, so this is our last full day here, and then we're leaving."

"That's too bad. I'd really like to get your input on a few details. However, Kelly and I will put our heads together. If we come up with anything new, you'll be the first one I call."

We chatted for several minutes longer. She informed me that Beau had already dropped off the hair samples with his guy. I felt blessed we'd met such nice people; I sensed a lifelong friendship forming. Coincidence or synchronicity?

Downstairs, Alexis was sitting by the fire. Joshua and Shadow, I was told, were in the playroom. She'd fed both of them.

"The guys are over at Peter's place already. They suggested maybe we meet at a place near the ski hill for breakfast. I told them we'd call once you're up."

I poured a cup of coffee and told Alexis about the phone call I'd had with Sam. She sat taller, listening to every detail.

With wide eyes, she asked, "What do you think? Could all this stuff actually be true?"

My shoulders lifted. "Who knows? I mean, both she and Kelly seem like genuine, reasonable people, right? I have a hard time *not* believing them. Plus, my intuition is fairly strong and I've had some intense feelings when we've been around the book and the drawing."

She nodded. "Yeah. I haven't said anything, but me too."

"Anyway, I told them today was probably too busy for us … packing and all … to fit in another visit. She'll call if they discover anything else."

"I'm sad today is the last day," she hung her head. "I don't want to pack."

Smiling at her, I felt her sadness. "Neither do I. And I certainly don't want to attend a funeral tomorrow. Why does it feel lately like I keep pulling out funeral clothing every couple of months? Sheesh!"

She smiled softly. "Because you have, dear."

"Well, I want to enjoy our last day here—it won't take long to pack this evening. Let's go join the guys for breakfast, at least."

* * *

When we walked in the front door of Peter's home, there was a small gathering in the hallway. Peter's parents were standing there; Greg, JJ, Hector, and Raj apparently had just joined them. Bill's look of disdain toward Shadow and Joshua was palpable. Maybe it wasn't such a good time.

"Well, hello Bill … Anne. Good to see you!" I gave them each a small hug and shot a questioning look to Greg over their shoulders. He shrugged. It was obvious they'd arrived only moments ahead of us.

Bill stated coldly, "Surprised you've all stuck around." He backed away from me and my pup abruptly.

Solemnly, my eyes cast downward before commenting. "We're leaving tomorrow morning. To attend the, uh, funeral."

Anne, who was wearing dark sunglasses, dabbed a tissue to her eyes and sniffled. "We're here to gather a few clothing items … for the funeral home. We thought it'd be nice if he had his favorite ski outfit." She burst into tears.

Greg asked, "Is there anything we can do for you?"

They both shook their heads. Then, Anne shared, "You haven't heard, have you?"

Greg immediately asked, "No, Anne, what's going on?"

"Well, the Albuquerque police picked up Tammi this morning. Michael is on the run."

There was a collective gasp. "What?" Greg was astonished.

Out of nowhere, Anne's anger surfaced beneath the tears. "I always knew she was trouble! That woman is a *gold digger!*"

I felt for Peter's mother. And none of this truly surprised me. I had similar feelings about the new bride, too. What was notable was how Anne had turned so quickly on Tammi. Days ago, she was singing her praises to whomever would listen.

Bill began pacing. "Well, Peter's mother is still quite

emotional about the news the police delivered this morning. I can't imagine Michael or Tammi being involved with Peter's death."

Greg stepped over to him. "We talked to the pilot the other day …"

"Whatever the hell for?" Bill spat. "You have no business inserting yourself into my son's death!"

Greg gasped, then held his hands up in surrender and backed away.

Raj attempted to calm Peter's father in the foyer, while Alexis shuffled Joshua out, and the rest of us awkwardly followed them to the kitchen.

Lexi nudged me. "What was that about? Is he always this nasty?"

I rolled my eyes. "In the few interactions I've had with him, I haven't exactly found him to be *nice*. And that was even before Peter's incident, during celebratory times."

"Michael is missing?" JJ asked.

"*Tammi's* in custody?" I emphasized.

Alexis pointed back to the living room where Raj and Bill had settled, and Hector joined them. "Go listen in," she prodded JJ. He nodded and left.

Greg was annoyed. "Why would he get so defensive about us speaking to the pilot? Last I checked, it was a free country." He paced around the kitchen irritably. Alexis and I took our seats on the stools.

Carefully, I tried comforting. "I don't know, honey, but please don't take it personally. They're not in the best mental state these days. We need to give them room for grief."

"Yeah? And I'm not grieving myself? They have some nerve…" He slammed a hand on the countertop, causing the rest of us to jump. Shaking his head, he looked up at me with tears forming in his eyes. "I'm sorry. But, Peter was *my friend*."

I walked over and put my arms around him. "I know, sweetie."

"None of this makes sense, Libby. I only want to understand how my friend died. He was an excellent skier. An outdoorsman who has trekked around the world. I don't understand how…"

"I know…"

Alexis gave us a sympathetic look. Then she asked us quietly, "Why was Tammi arrested, I wonder?"

We pulled away from each other and turned to her. I looked back at Greg. "That's true; sounds like the police have ventured away from 'accidental death' if Tammi was arrested. We need to learn more."

"Listen, guys …" Lexi started, looking down at Joshua standing next to her. "It's gotten quite serious here with Peter's parents having arrived. I'm going to take him back to our place. This may not be the best place for us right now."

I nodded in agreement, and pulled out her keys. She went over to JJ, whispered in his ear, and then she and her son left quietly. Apparently, JJ wanted to stay, as he hadn't moved from his observation spot in the living room.

Soon after Alexis left, we quietly went back to the group. I sat on a far sofa with Shadow at my feet. Greg joined Hector on the large sofa closest to the family members. Bill and Raj were talking about the company, it seemed.

"They have no idea what they are talking about!" Bill grumped.

Raj agreed, then calmly stated, "Well, you and I know

that. But our experts are still trying to convince the regulators. It takes time."

"There is no time! My son's dead. Michael is nowhere around. The company is in dire straits." He stood, stomped away, and stopped with his back to us, looking out the windows.

I took the quiet moment to ask, "Have they actually charged Tammi? What exactly is she accused of?"

Everyone turned to look at me. Anne stood up and joined her husband at the window.

Raj and Hector answered at the same time. Raj signaled for Hector to go ahead.

"No charges yet. They are questioning her, though. They apparently discovered that Tammi purchased a life insurance policy worth ten million dollars on Peter, a week before the wedding. And, er, his death."

"Okay. That doesn't mean anything, does it?"

"Well, I guess there are also some holes in her alibi. The day Peter went missing, she's changed her story several times about her exact location. Also, the police are following a claim from a known criminal who has come forward saying someone tried to hire him—to murder Peter. He didn't take the job. But, that leaves so many questions: who tried to hire him? Did they ultimately hire someone else? Who *wanted* Peter dead?"

My memory flashed to seeing Tammi from the ski lift the day of his disappearance. The time frame didn't match up, but who was she with? Also, I knew at some point later, she'd been seen on camera in front of Sweet's Sweets.

"There are still details the police aren't divulging, but it's apparent they think she conspired to have him killed."

"Holy! What on earth?" Greg exclaimed.

I was still a little confused. "But, hadn't they told us he died of hypothermia? Exposure to the elements? How does that fit in with a hired hitman?"

Bill turned around. Calmer now, he said, "Well, of course, they'd find hypothermia. His body was out in the elements for days." Anne sniffled, but continued staring out the window. "The official autopsy results are still pending, though. No one is sure how it all fits in."

I nodded. "Okay. Well, this latest news from the police fits with what we learned in Santa Fe…"

Bill turned back toward the window.

Raj nodded. "Good point, Libby. The pilot stated Peter wasn't alone. Perhaps the police *have been* investigating that angle all along—and found this other passenger?"

I could tell that Bill and Anne were listening, even though they'd ceased engaging for the moment. Grief aside, I couldn't help but wonder why they were so defensive of everyone's theories. Denial perhaps.

Greg snapped his fingers. "Long blonde hair. Isn't that how Will—the pilot—described the person?"

Raj nodded. "I sort of had the image it was a lady friend," he said, with caution in front of Peter's parents. "And from what Will said, it seemed Peter knew his passenger. That doesn't sound like a hitman to me."

I shrugged. "Keep your enemies close … Maybe Peter knew the person? Made him an easier target?"

"Oh, all this is preposterous!" Bill turned around, shouting. "Tammi didn't hire a hit man!"

Anne chuckled. "She's a gold digger, Bill. I've told you this from the beginning."

"Okay. What about Michael? Why is he on the run? Any theories?" I asked, looking around the room to see who would jump in first.

Silence filled the room.

"Is it possible that Michael and Tammi were working together to get rid of Peter?" I suggested. *Was it Michael with Tammi that day on the ski hill?* I thought.

Bill and Anne talked over one another, denying that could *ever* happen. Raj and Hector shook their heads vehemently, but weren't vocal. JJ sat back, taking in all the simultaneous reactions.

Greg jumped when the phone rang in his pocket. He pulled it out to take the call, mouthing 'my mom' to me as he left the room. I sat back, listening to everyone's theories, and exchanging perplexed glances with JJ often.

Bill, Raj, and Hector turned the conversation toward the health of the company now with the FDA investigation and the lawsuits. Bill felt this was the undoing of Michael, and that was a motive for him to disappear. Raj and Hector disagreed; the company was Michael's baby, and he'd defend it to the end. Anne kept rambling that the correct person was in police custody; everything had fallen apart since she came into Peter's life.

Greg stepped back into the room and whispered for me to join him outside. I grabbed Shadow's leash, and we followed him out into the frosty sunshine. That's where he dropped the bomb.

"Larry was the one skiing with Peter that day. He just came forward to the family and police today."

Greg's brother was the hitman?

CHAPTER TWENTY-TWO

What did this mean? That was the only question repeating itself in my brain as I stared at Greg. *His brother Larry was with Peter.* Okay, I could see Larry and Peter going to the backcountry—from their shared love of dangerous adventures, particularly skiing—that made sense. *Long blonde hair—was it a match for the hair found in the helicopter?* But the part that settled like a heavy weight on my heart: *why hadn't Larry been immediately forthright about the expedition? Wait, where had he been since that day?* I struggled to remember anything about his whereabouts in the days after Peter's disappearance.

Greg's voice surfaced again in my consciousness. How much had I missed? "He told our parents that he'd been partying with some ladies … he only learned last night that

Peter had died. That's when he told them over the phone. My mom and dad are struggling—."

"So, he hadn't known Peter never came off the mountain?"

"Well, hopefully he'll fill us in on that later. He apparently seemed as surprised as any of us to learn of Peter's death."

"Wait. Why haven't any of us questioned where Larry was all this time? Had you realized he hasn't been around?"

Greg shook his head shamefully. "Honestly, no. It's all been a whirlwind now … I can't tell you. The police are still questioning him, so we may learn more later."

"This is unbelievable!" Then I considered how Greg must feel. This was *his brother*. How could his brother be responsible for Peter's death? "I'm so sorry this is happening to your family. I'm sure there is a perfectly good explanation, right?"

He shrugged, clearly upset and considering what was next. "Well, the Schulls are going to learn this information any time now, so I might as well go break the news myself." We ambled up the steps to the front door. We heard the melee before we opened the door.

Anne, Bill, and Raj were standing up, all pointing fingers at one another. JJ stood off to one side, ready to jump in to stop it all. Hector was across the room pacing back and forth, but seemingly enjoying the show.

"Whoa! What's going on?" Greg hollered.

None of them stopped to notice Greg.

Hector stopped Greg from breaking them up. "Dude, so much dirty laundry is being aired. Let them go. This is good."

"Michael and Peter were not considering dissolving the company!" Raj shouted in answer to Bill's accusation.

"Where do you get this stuff?"

Shadow barked and finally drew everyone's attention away from the argument.

"Get that dog out of my son's house!" Bill yelled, pointing to the front door.

Greg stepped forward. "Bill. Please calm down."

"Calm down? Don't tell me…"

Greg held his ground, touching the side of the older gentlemen's arm. "Bill. I have something to tell you and I need you to please sit down."

He and Anne complied, sitting in the closest chairs. Anne grabbed for the tissue in her pocket. I'd never seen someone quickly switch her emotions so broadly.

"Bill. Anne. My parents called. Uh, they have informed me that my brother was with Peter the day he died."

"Well, yeah, they all went skiing that morning…" Bill said. He paused, then looked directly at Greg. "Oh, you mean to say that Larry was with our son in the backcountry? On the expedition!" His voice got progressively louder with his comprehension.

JJ saw what was about to occur and moved closer to Greg's side. Shadow and I moved into the kitchen. Anne began blubbering.

Bill's face turned bright red. He stood, pointing his finger at Greg's chest. "YOU mean to tell ME *your* BROTHER has been responsible all along?!" he screamed. As he took a step forward, JJ used his bulk to separate the two.

"Okay, man … you need to back off," JJ grunted. "Nothing gets solved this way and you know it. Please sit."

"Look, Bill … I only learned this information minutes ago. I knew nothing prior. And, quite frankly, we still don't know all the details. I have no idea whether Larry is responsible for Peter's death, but I find it highly unlikely."

Anne blew her nose, continuing to sob.

"Where is he now? I need to talk to that punk!" Bill ordered, as he stormed toward the front door.

"He's at the police station. Let's wait to hear from the police," Greg tried to reason.

The front door slammed.

* * *

Our group left the Schull household, leaving Raj to deal with Anne. Along with Hector, we picked up Alexis and Joshua and headed to the restaurant we'd planned for breakfast earlier. There were so many unanswered questions and we needed time to process everything without all the Schull's drama.

"I'm guessing we're going to learn the long blonde hair was Larry's then," I added, while taking a bite of my veggie omelet.

Alexis and JJ nodded.

Hector looked questioningly at the rest of us. "What hair?"

Greg filled Hector in on the conversation that he'd tried earlier to have with Bill. He explained everything we learned from our visit with the pilot in Santa Fe.

Alexis and I were at the far end of the rectangular table, so while the guys were talking, she nudged me. "That call from Sam earlier ..." she looked up to be sure she wasn't overheard. "How do you think this newest information fits in with that illustration?"

"Oh, so you *do* think that drawing could lead us to

solving this mystery?" I teased. "Honestly, I hadn't thought any more about it. Other than hoping Sam finds the person responsible for the vandalism."

"Remember the skiing scenes, though. What if there's something there that could prove Larry wasn't involved?"

"But leaving your buddy in a dangerous situation still holds him culpable, doesn't it? Hiding it from the authorities makes that even worse," I pointed out.

"True. I wonder what happened."

My phone vibrated in my pocket. I retrieved and answered it. Alexis watched intently as I gave the typical "uh, huh," "yeah," then said goodbye and hung up.

"Well?" she said impatiently.

Looking toward the guys, I could see they were deep in conversation and hadn't even noticed me on the phone. I leaned in and whispered, "It was Sam. She was in a hurry, but wanted to let us know that the hair belonged to a Lawrence Lawson. Exactly as we now suspected, only I had hoped I'd been wrong."

"Oh, boy. This really doesn't look good for Larry, does it?"

"Well, no different from before we knew this bit. I mean, he's saying he was there … so the hair evidence makes sense. And, at least it doesn't add yet another person to the mix. However, none of it answers questions about a hitman or where Larry's been since."

"Larry's confession may get Tammi off the hook," she added.

"I don't know. Guess more has to be learned about murder for hire. How did the authorities come to that conclusion?"

"I wonder if you'd be able to visit Greg's ex-girlfriend

in jail when you're in Albuquerque?"

I looked at her in shock. "Why would I do that?"

"To learn more…"

"And you think she'd tell *me*?"

She shrugged. Anything was possible.

Greg caught my attention and indicated he'd already paid for the meal. Everyone bundled up in their layers and we left.

* * *

When Greg's parents arrived, he and I met them in Taos, at the police station. The Johnson family stayed at the house. Perhaps they'd get in a little more skiing before packing up.

When we walked into the lobby of the station, Greg's parents were sitting on pleather chairs. They stood as we approached; I hugged both of them and offered sympathies. I couldn't imagine what they were going through.

Greg asked, "Are we going to meet with him?"

Gene nodded. "His attorney is meeting us here. I'm hopeful we can bail him out."

"Wait, I'm confused. He's been *charged*? With what?"

"You're right, son—my bad. He is only being questioned. I only meant we're here to pick him up and take him home."

"Maybe then he'll open up with us," Betsy added.

"Are you headed back to Pagosa Springs today, then?"

"No, we rented a place for tonight. Tomorrow we'll go to Albuquerque for the services, then we'll head home," Gene explained.

The morning was still young when we learned that

they'd only allow Larry's attorney and parents in to see him right now. We waited long enough to learn that the process would take a while, so we admitted defeat and decided to make better use of our time.

Walking down a long corridor to leave the jail, I halted.

"What's wrong?" Greg asked.

"Look—it's Sarah," I pointed into the room we'd stopped next to. His expression reminded me he hadn't been there at the bakery contest. "That lady ... we think she vandalized Sam's shop."

"Oh? Well, she's in cuffs. Looks like there may be accountability after all."

We turned a corner and nearly ran right into Tammi.

CHAPTER TWENTY-THREE

The police officer leading her down the hallway apologized to us, and gently pulled her away as she stood with her mouth gaping open, but saying nothing.

"Tammi—" I said.

"Ma'am, move along," the officer ushered Tammi along.

Her eyes looked pleadingly at Greg. Neither of us could find any words.

They disappeared around another corner and we made our way out the front doors.

"Where was her attorney? I sure hope she has one," I said, as Greg held the door open for me. "Maybe JJ can make some calls?"

"Apparently the law has caught up to her finally, and

maybe we should stay out of it," Greg stated. "I mean, of course she needs fair representation, but … I'm sorry, I don't think a tiger changes its stripes. Even after this many years."

I left it at that for now. It seemed to me since the police quickly extradited her to this jurisdiction, there must be something to their accusations. Maybe Greg was right.

Once we were in the car, pulling out of the police parking lot, I asked, "Can we stop at the bakery? I'd like to see if Samantha is there."

Several minutes later, we pulled up in front of the cute shop. There was a line forming out the door. I peeked into the display window and saw Jen busily helping fulfill orders from the pastry case. Sam walked in from the backroom with a large pan of muffins to fill the case. She looked up and saw us. Her hand went up and signaled to us to come in.

We squeezed through the crowd and Sam shepherded us into the kitchen.

"So good to see you guys!" she hugged each of us. "Be right back. Let me get those muffins in their place really quick."

She shuffled off.

Becky called out from across a worktable. "Hey guys! Good to see you again. How'd you all enjoy that cake?"

I stumbled for a moment. We'd forgotten all about it. The cake was so beautiful and we had displayed it on the countertop, but then with everything else going on, I wondered—had the Johnsons cut into it yet? I couldn't say. Instead of admitting that, I replied, "It was delicious!" I'm sure that wasn't a lie.

"You're probably leaving Taos soon, I'm guessing?"

she asked, spreading a buttercream expertly onto a two-layer round cake.

"Yes, tomorrow, unfortunately." I left out the part about the funeral. "We've had a great time exploring around here. Taos is a special town. Sam and Kelly were great, giving us a tour and all."

Sam made her reappearance. Her energy was infectious. "Guess what happened?"

"They got her!" I exclaimed.

Her face drooped. "How'd you know?"

"We just came from the police station."

"What were you doing there?"

"Long story …" I looked at Greg, unsure whether he wanted me airing his family business.

He nodded, then added, "My brother is there for questioning."

"Ohhh. Need me to talk to Beau—is there something we can do?" she sweetly offered.

Greg shook his head. "No, no. My parents and their lawyer are there. Fingers crossed he'll be out today."

"Do you mind my asking … what's happening?"

He and I exchanged nervous glances. Then I said, "Remember Greg's friend I told you about who died this week? Well…"

Sam's hands immediately cover her mouth. "Oh dear. You're not saying…"

"No, he didn't kill Peter," Greg was adamant about that. "But, he was one of the last people to see him alive. Therefore, the police have questions. Heck, *I* have questions—he never told us."

Sam looked at me. "We should consult the drawing."

Confused, Greg's eyebrows lifted. I whispered, "I'll

explain later."

To Sam, "Is the drawing here? I'd love to see it."

"Yes, I brought it with me today. With Sarah's arrest, I wondered what changes might be unveiled."

She may as well have sprouted horns; my face twisted in confusion. "Hold on. This illustration *changes* with the circumstances?"

She nodded with a mysterious grin.

How on earth was that possible? I thought.

"C'mon, follow me," she guided us through the kitchen to her desk. "Look." She had the drawing spread out on her desk.

I gasped. The bakery was no longer there. The two women … gone. Now, that segment of the illustration was replaced with what appeared to be a police station. No, *two* police stations. I noticed the ski hill portion of the picture had changed as well. *Where was that strange word? Memu… something or another.* My eyes carefully scanned over each sketching. It was so different from the last time I saw it.

"Can I take a picture of this?" I asked Sam. "There's so much to take in."

"Sure."

After I put my phone back into my pocket, Kelly walked in.

"I see Mom's told you … isn't that wild?"

"Honestly, none of this seems real. Are you sure this is the same drawing? Or did Ana draw a new one?"

"No, it's the exact same paper …"

I couldn't explain it and my head hurt trying to rationalize. However, something in my gut told me we weren't looking at this correctly. Not the picture necessarily, but the whole situation with Peter.

CHAPTER TWENTY-FOUR

Not even eleven o'clock yet, and I felt like my head was spinning with all this new information. Larry, Sarah, and Tammi were all at the police station. Peter's service was planned for tomorrow. His father was flipping out—ok, so was his mother, understandably. Michael was nowhere to be found. *Were Tammi and Larry in cahoots? Or, Tammi and Michael? And, why had Tammi's aunt vandalized the bakery?* If Sam was correct, *how were the two incidents connected?*

I understood why Sam and Kelly would think there's a connection. Otherwise, why would the skiers appear in the same drawing as the bakery's security footage? That made sense to me. What I couldn't rationalize was the whole concept of the drawing itself, and its ever-changing updates. That was bizarre. Still, there was something lingering in my consciousness that told me to trust—even if nothing made sense.

By the time we made it back to the house, Alexis was putting lunch together, using the remaining food in the refrigerator. She offered to make us some grilled cheese sandwiches.

I sat next to Joshua at the breakfast bar; Greg headed to our suite, saying he was going to pack his suitcase.

"So? Did you learn anything new?" Alexis asked.

"The authorities have extradited Tammi."

"Whoa, already?" she exclaimed. "That seems fast!"

"Exactly as I was thinking. We actually ran into her in the hallway."

"Did you guys get to talk to her … or Larry?"

I shook my head. "Greg's parents are there; it's going to be awhile. I've invited them over later, but there's no telling how long the questioning will go on."

Greg and JJ came into the kitchen after smelling the aroma of toasted cheese. We sat around the breakfast bar and ate our sandwiches. Shadow caught anything that hit the floor. I noticed she'd strategically placed herself below Joshua.

"I don't wanna leave…" Joshua pouted.

"None of us do, sweetie," I told him. "What was your favorite part?"

"Gingerbread!"

"Really? Even over skiing?" JJ asked.

"Skiing!" he exclaimed.

We all laughed. He kept shouting favorites and told us how he loved his new friend, Ana. So sweet. The funniest part came later, after we'd moved into the living room. He was playing on the floor with Shadow when he asked her about her favorite part of the trip. He leaned in, whispering, then let her lick him all over his face. She got charged up, started the zoomies around the room and barked at Joshua. After a few minutes of that, she flopped down, panting, and staring at Joshua.

"She said her favorite part was us!" he danced around. "Her Christmas wish was to spend lots and lots of time with US! And get all the cookies she could!"

The two of them got wild again, so we ushered them into the playroom to reduce the risk of breaking something on the final day of our trip. The rest of us decided it was time to pack and get started cleaning up; we'd go have one last nice dinner out before we left early the next morning.

Greg's phone vibrated, and he answered it. When he finally hung up, he let us know that his parents and Larry would join us around dinner time.

* * *

During dinner at a wonderful steak restaurant at the base of the ski hill, we listened to Larry's tale of what happened. That became fruitless. It was difficult for everyone to hear much detail, and we didn't want to shout questions in the public setting. We decided once we were done with the meal, we'd gather back at our rental for after-dinner coffee or drinks instead.

Once back at the house, Alexis got Joshua settled in the playroom with his favorite video game. Shadow, of course, stuck right by his side.

Greg sat across from his brother. "I don't understand where you've been since..."

Larry ran his hands over his scalp, through his long

hair, and exhaled. "I know. I know." He stood up and walked around the room. "I feel so responsible now that I know he *died* up there. Geez, I had no idea!" He looked around the room; his dad gave him a nod to continue. "Oh, God … Greg, this is hard to admit."

"I'm listening…" Greg said patiently.

"Tammi and I had something going," he blurted out. "A long time ago," he clarified.

We stayed quiet, urging him to say more.

"It was a while ago, but after seeing her again that first night we arrived … well, all the feelings surfaced again." He hung his head for a second. "I knew she was getting married. I was actually happy for her, and didn't expect to feel anything. It surprised me when I learned she was marrying your college friend, but hey, no worries."

He explained that during the first couple of nights' parties, she kept flirting. They were both drunk, and they ended up making out. Once he sobered up, he was so confused. He questioned her about continuing with the wedding. She couldn't care less about his concerns, he said. At least, that was his perception. Earlier in the day that Peter went missing, he had found Tammi skiing on her own, so he caught up to her and wanted to talk.

He was the one that I saw with her!

Larry left, fairly upset, determined to tell Peter himself. He called Peter, who had left the group before lunch, and discovered that he had organized a backcountry adventure on his own. He was currently in his SUV, getting ready to head to the Taos airport.

"He encouraged me to join him last minute. I was unsure—but wanted to be upfront with him and needed to talk. Plus, the adventure sounded really cool…" his sheepish smile crept in. "I hefted my skis out to the parking lot; he picked me up, and off we went."

"You didn't tell anyone else in the group?" I asked.

"No. Hadn't thought about it, really … and they weren't around, anyway. Everyone was off skiing, grabbing lunch, or whatever they were doing. I don't know."

The story after that matched what the pilot had previously told us. Peter showed up at the airport with an unexpected guest. Larry told us he could sense the pilot wasn't happy about it, so Larry quietly stepped aside while they worked out the arrangements. Once they'd taken off, it's not as though he could talk to Peter easily, or privately, so he remained quiet and let the pilot and Peter talk throughout the flight. The backcountry area wasn't far away, but not available to the public without permitting.

"Once the helicopter flew away, and before we set off, I told Peter about Tammi." Larry sat down on a chair; his head facing down shamefully. "I let him know Tammi had come on to me. I was drunk…" he stood, now agitated. "How stupid can I get?!"

He walked around while lamenting the fact that he told Peter anything at all. Explaining what happened next, he became angrier.

"Peter got right in my face and told me she'd never leave him for me. I am nothing; he's the only one who can give Tammi the life she deserves. He told me to 'get over it' with his trademark wealthy smug smile. I was so hurt and angry. At who? Myself, mostly. Not Peter. Ok, yes, and I was really upset and hurt by *Tammi*. But, never Peter … even the way he treated me right then."

"What happened next?" Greg asked.

"I skied away," he stated matter-of-factly. "I only

wanted to get away from him."

"That's dangerous terrain—you two didn't ski together?"

"Nah. Before we ever got to the airport, we'd already decided not to slow each other. We'd meet at the bottom; adventure of a lifetime—that was the plan all along, man."

"So, where did you go then?" I asked.

He sighed loudly. His posture again showed shame, with his shoulders slumped farther, and his eyes cast downward, looking at the floor.

"I was upset. When I got to the bottom of the hill, I went back to my rental, changed my clothes, and headed into town to a bar. I got tanked."

"But you *never* came back this whole week …" Greg stated. Their dad nodding along with that.

Larry looked at his mom, clearly not wanting to divulge more in front of her. But he eventually continued. "Look, I'm not proud of myself, alright. I got stupid drunk … maybe some other substances, too," he muttered the last part under his breath, avoiding eye contact with his mother. "And uh, well, I met someone. Er, okay, maybe a *couple* of nice ladies. One thing led to another, and I stayed at their place for several days."

"And only yesterday you learned about Peter's demise?" I asked.

"Yeah … they actually lived in Tierra Amarilla. Oh, forty-five minutes away maybe—but a really nice place in the country. No TV." He looked up sheepishly again, then said, "Well, there could have been a TV, but we never turned it on. Uh, we kept … busy."

"Did the police believe this story?" Greg asked, looking at his parents. "And what about you two—why not question where Larry was all week?"

Gene cleared his throat. "First, we had no reason for concern. Larry had called us that afternoon—the day we're talking about here. He told us he'd met up with friends and he'd see us back in Pagosa. That's Larry; never in one place for long. We did not know he'd been skiing with Peter that day, though." He took another sip of his wine before continuing. "Our attorney believes Larry's alibi will hold up. They found the, uh, *ladies*. So long as they can account for all the time they spent with Larry, then I think he'll be just fine."

"I still can't believe you and Peter separated," Betsy quietly added. "That was extremely dangerous, son."

"I'm mortified that he never made it down. Still in shock over that … he was such a great skier, I never considered he wouldn't make it down. I do feel so responsible for not being a better friend. In several ways. Had I been there, maybe…" He lowered his head again and sobs overtook him. His mother moved over and put her arms around him.

We spent the rest of the evening getting Larry caught up on everything that'd happened all week long. Everyone shared theories about what happened to Peter, but we were still in the same predicament—no one knew for sure.

CHAPTER TWENTY-FIVE

We said our goodbyes to the Johnsons early the next morning, and each went our separate ways. The journey to Albuquerque took roughly two hours. We'd prearranged to leave Shadow with Raj's extended family while we attended the services.

Several of Greg's friends and their families were standing outside the doors to the church when we walked up. We hugged Hector, and he introduced us to his wife and children. She explained they missed the wedding because of prior commitments. The children with sports and his wife being a busy attorney in Los Angeles, where they live. Greg's parents attended, but Dana and Larry had not. She had her hands full with the kids; he felt it was inappropriate to be there and was still ashamed of his role in the incident, so he left for home when his parents headed to Albuquerque. Then, I saw Tammi and her sister, Abby, walking inside. *They released her?*

The ushers escorted us to our seats close to the front with the family and friends. Once everyone took their seats, I looked behind and noticed people standing at the back. I looked all over for Tammi, but couldn't locate her. She wasn't sitting anywhere near the Schulls in the front row, that was for certain. And thank God.

The sanctuary was packed full. I pulled out a few tissues, bracing myself for a very emotional ceremony. When it was all over, I'd used every tissue I had.

Outside of the church, I stood watching the attendees filing out. Greg was deep in conversation with several people he knew. That's when I spotted the twins. I casually walked across the front lawn and approached them.

"Tammi. I'm so sorry for your loss," I said, as though I knew nothing of the accusations against her. "Is there anything that Greg or I can do?"

"I think that family has done enough, thank you," she rudely said, and turned away.

I reached out for her arm, only trying to get her attention. Abby swiftly blocked me. "Wait. I don't know what you mean. I only …"

"The Lawsons can explain precisely who caused my husband's death," she yelled, loud enough for several bystanders to hear. "Larry killed Peter!" she screamed.

Now everyone looked in our direction. Greg noticed me with them and came running, followed by Bill Schull.

Tammi continued her tirade, turning beet red, and tears streaming down her face. Shocked, I didn't know how to respond—or how to quiet her down.

"Tammi, I know about what happened with Larry earlier this week …"

Her head whipped around. "What do you think you know?" she spat.

"Larry confessed and told the police that you and he had a thing … and that it continued prior to the wedding."

She didn't deny anything, but only paused for a second. Then, she launched herself at me, long nails and all. "He killed Peter! Up on that mountain!" she screamed.

Greg and Bill pulled her off of me. They walked her out to the parking lot; she and Abby got into a car and squealed away. By the time the men returned, a group had gathered.

"How is she out of jail, anyway?" I heard one person ask.

"Yikes, how awkward … and disrespectful to the family," another commented.

Greg took me in his arms. "I'm sorry about that."

"Not your fault," I mumbled, still listening to people's remarks.

"What did you say to her?" Greg asked me.

"I gave my condolences and asked how we could help," I scoffed. "She launched with remarks that 'your family had already done enough'."

He grimaced. Bill walked over and asked if I was okay. It was the nicest he'd been the entire time I'd known him.

"How did she get released?" I asked him.

"That's precisely what I'm going to find out. We had no idea."

Greg's family walked up, asked about me, and then we walked to the parking lot together.

"How does Tammi even know about Larry's involvement, if no one knew he'd been with Peter skiing?" I asked the Lawson family collectively. No one knew.

Raj's family had been so kind as to offer their home for the reception. They had an immense property on the far northeast end of the city. Although chilly, the midday sun shone brightly. It was comfortable enough outside—there were also heaters available to keep us warm. We milled around, visiting with guests and indulging ourselves with appetizers. Shadow loved the large enclosed area and already had made herself at home while we'd been away.

My phone buzzed in my purse. I stepped aside when I saw it was Kelly calling; Shadow followed my every move.

"Libby—have you left Taos?" she asked.

"Hi Kelly! Yes," I quieted my voice, "we're at Peter's funeral."

"Oh geez, sorry for the call then," she responded in hushed tones, too.

"No worries. We're actually at the reception now—and I'm outside. Whatcha need?"

"I wanted to show you another version of the *picture* ... oh, wait, I can take a photo." I heard her shuffling around. "There. I sent you a photo of the drawing. It's changed again!"

I looked at my display and saw her text come through. I tapped the photo, then used two fingers to zoom in. Where the bakery once was ... and then the police stations ... now, there was a home with a sprawling lawn, many people gathered, and... I caught my breath. "Oh God!" I gasped, looking around my current location.

"You got it … are you looking at the photo?" Kelly asked.

"Oh, yes … sorry. Kelly. I think I'm at this home in the picture."

"You're kidding me!" She began repeating what I told her. I assumed Sam was there.

"Put me on speaker phone—if that's your mom," I said.

"Hi Libby," Sam's familiar voice sounded. "We were wondering why the police stations had disappeared from the drawing."

"I think I know." My trepidation had to be heard at their end. "They have released Tammi. We saw her at the funeral earlier."

"You're kidding," Kelly said.

"I wonder what's happened to her aunt?" Sam uttered at the same time.

Shadow barked. I looked down and gave her a shush.

They were right—*both* police stations had been replaced on the illustration. *What did that mean? And why the reception location?* If that indeed was the intent from the drawing.

"Libby, we're going to go. Beau can find out if they have released Sarah. We'll call you when we know more. In the meantime, watch your back … and Greg, too."

"You think *we* are in danger?" I asked, cautiously.

"No, not necessarily. But—well, we don't know what the message is. Let's just say I'm not comfortable with the fact that it appears you're in the newest drawing's scene."

Exactly why I was unnerved.

We hung up, and I rejoined Greg, who was now in deep conversation with Hector. I found myself half listening, and mostly paranoid, watching everyone's movements.

Peter's parents had finally made it to the gathering and were talking to Greg's parents. I saw many people I'd never seen before. For one, Raj's family was enormous, and I saw them milling about everywhere, making sure everyone had what they needed. But also, I assumed the crowd included many who Peter worked with over the years.

Country music played as background music. Someone commented that it was Peter's playlist. Then, Hector's voice got excitable, but not in a good way. My attention went back to their conversation. Greg had asked more about the trials related to the diabetes device. Hector became somewhat defensive while discussing it. I imagined that had to do with the investigation. Not long into the explanation, all eyes moved toward the side gate we'd walked in through earlier. Shadow barked and ran across the lawn.

Michael walked through, closing the gate behind him.

CHAPTER TWENTY-SIX

Where have you been, man?" Greg was the first one to reach him, grabbing Shadow and pulling her back. She showed an uncharacteristic agitation. I quickly retrieved her leash and moved her away as all of Michael's friends swarmed him.

"It's a long story …" he said. Then he turned to the man who'd walked up behind him.

Bill interrupted. "Son. No explanations are needed. Come enjoy this celebration of life. We're so happy you have joined us."

Greg looked dejected. We exchanged an eye roll and decided we'd catch up with Michael later. We both wanted to know why he was considered 'on the lam'. *Was it even true the police were looking for Michael? Were Raj's family now unknowingly harboring a fugitive?* And, *what got Shadow all worked up?*

My phone rang. Sam this time.

"Libby—another change. A man, standing in shadows. I've got to say, there sure is an ominous look to the scene; the beautiful garden setting has darkened now. Oh, and the ski hills are gone. Wait, there is … *an angel appearing?*" she reported, clearly awestruck. "I have no idea…"

Chills overtook me. My heart raced. The only thought that came was—Michael. *But, why?*

She said they'd send me the photo. I hung up.

Greg leaned in. "Who was that?"

"Sam. I'll call her back." I knew he didn't share the same belief on spell books or the illustration so I kept that to myself for now. "I need to find a restroom. Do you know where it is?"

We went on the search and I tried keeping my anxiety tempered so as not to draw attention to myself.

We found the bathroom, and Greg took Shadow's leash. "Please don't let her loose. She seems anxious with everyone around."

"Yeah, with Michael around," he laughed. "We're going to walk out front for a bit, away from everyone."

I nodded before closing the door behind me. Inside the bathroom, I let my guard down. I'd been completely rattled by the appearance of Michael … but why? Shadow's reaction, for one. Whether I believed in Ana's drawing was beside the point now. My dog's intuition was always spot on. But what did that mean—*was Michael somehow responsible for Peter's death?* I presumed, after Larry's alibi, that Peter's death had to be linked to Tammi. Or, of course, truly an accidental death. *What was Michael's role in it?*

I quickly pulled my phone out of my purse and found

the newest text message. Sam had already sent three. Zooming in, I saw what she'd mentioned. The picture was completely different. No ski hills, a darker background. The home and landscape had changed, and centered in the middle now was, as Sam accurately described, an ominous man. The detail was amazing. Alarmingly, my instincts were correct—there was no doubt about it. The image was Michael. Tall, dark clothing, and the telltale sign were the company logo sunglasses. *Identical to Peter's.*

My attention was drawn to the top half of the page. Again, in exquisite detail, and as Sam described, there was an angel overlooking the scene. *What did this mean?*

The phone chimed. Another text, and I quickly opened the latest image.

Mostly, it was identical to the last one. Only when I zoomed in on the other side of the house, I saw a man and a dog.

I shoved the phone into my purse and ran from the bathroom.

Navigating the hallway, then the kitchen, where I dodged several women carrying large trays of food, I ran for the front door. My phone chimed again. Ignoring it, I ran outside looking for Greg and Shadow.

I shielded my eyes and blinked when I stepped out into the bright sunlight. Looking left, then right … they were nowhere around. I ran down the steps and onto the long driveway, quickly scanning my surroundings. Just then, Greg and Shadow emerged from the side of the house, out from around some bushes.

"Hey, you found us!" he said, searching his pockets. "I forgot a bag … we need …"

Movement caught my periphery; police vehicles approached.

Before Greg finished his sentence, he looked up and also saw the three vehicles that had stopped twenty yards away. "What's going on?" he asked.

I shrugged. We both watched as six officers exited the vehicles. Two of them headed toward the side gate entry. Two approached the front door. The remaining officers approached us.

"Libby Madsen?"

"Yes," I answered, shocked. *How did they know me?*

The officer greeted Shadow nicely by name.

"But—" I started.

"We're looking for Michael Thorn. We got a call from Kelly Porter … on your behalf, saying he was at this location."

Greg and I stood there, stunned.

"We're going to need to take a statement from both of you. Don't go anywhere."

There was a commotion and all four of us turned to look.

Two officers had Michael in cuffs, hauling him to their vehicle. Bill followed, shouting expletives and demanding answers. Immediately, the other two officers surrounded him with warnings to back off. The one police car left with Michael in it, and the rest of the officers began taking statements from all the guests.

Raj's family, who had kindly opened their home for all these strangers, did not know of Michael's wrongdoings. They hadn't even known he was on their premises.

As Bill continued his belligerence, the police invited the Schulls to go downtown to speak with them and swiftly removed them from the home.

Greg, his parents, and I all gave statements. Which, ultimately, amounted to very little. I couldn't tell them about the drawings or I'd end up in a mental hospital. And I did not know how Kelly knew about Michael.

During the process, we learned Michael was wanted because of their business lawsuit. It had nothing to do with Peter's death. That left me floundering. *Then what was the message from Ana's ever-adapting illustration?*

Then, I remembered Tammi was free and still blamed Larry.

CHAPTER TWENTY-SEVEN

We found ourselves back at the original hotel we stayed in at the beginning of our vacation. Minus the Johnsons this time, of course. As soon as we checked in, I took Shadow for a walk around the neighborhood and thought about the next steps. My only desire now was to spend a quiet evening with my partner and pup, and with my focus homed in on finally reaching Arizona.

However, my mind kept going back to that darned illustration. Prior to this afternoon, the etching depicted scenes that had already happened. *That seemed to have changed now*, I thought, remembering how I could see Greg and Shadow on their walk. That still frightened me because the feeling of the picture was so ominous.

If Peter's death was an accident, then why the police

concern about Tammi, Michael, Larry—or Sarah, for that matter? Shadow and I walked around the last corner before heading back to our hotel. It came to me: I didn't believe that Peter's death was an accident. I agreed with Greg—we already knew, from the initial sheriff's report, that there were no obvious signs of trauma. No broken limbs, and he hadn't bled to death. Had Tammi hired a hitman, wouldn't there be bullet wounds? So, what prevented him from getting down that mountain? *That's exactly why I can't let this go.*

We found Greg coming out of the lobby doors as we passed by. I looked questioningly.

"Maintenance is going to come look at our door. It's all askew, and the lock doesn't fit properly."

"Thanks. I hadn't noticed that."

"Hey, is Tammi staying at Peter's still? Which I guess technically is 'theirs' anyway…" I asked.

"I have no idea where she is."

"I'd like to talk to her. We're missing something. The police released her; that has to indicate they don't have enough evidence to hold her, right? That must have been what the interview in Taos was about. Interesting that they actually drove her there for that."

Greg reached his limit. "I say we drop this whole thing. Peter's dead. His service is over. There's nothing that will bring him back. No, I don't believe it was an accident any more than you do, but we have to leave it up to the police. Let's rest, then tackle the drive home tomorrow. I'm ready to be done."

I could see it etched in his face, through his shoulders—he was tired. He was probably right. What more could we do, anyway?

"Are you hungry? We only had a few appetizers, hours ago," I asked.

"I could eat. What are you thinking about?"

"Thai food," I nudged.

"That sounds perfect."

Greg's phone rang. "Hector," he said, then answered it.

I fed Shadow, and she went into her kennel.

When he hung up, Greg announced Hector suggested a great place. And he'd join us. I had been looking forward to having an evening with Greg all to myself, so I found myself annoyed momentarily. I liked Hector, though. Only one more night.

He was waiting for us outside the front doors of Orchid Thai, and greeted us warmly.

"This place doesn't look like much from the outside, but wait till you taste the food," Hector raved, as a car nearby squealed its tires and sped off down the road. "Geez! Let's get inside…" he held the door open for us.

We walked in and it was beautiful. Bamboo all along the walls, a nice water feature, and cozy dining setting. After the hostess took us to our seats in the far corner, we settled with our drinks and relaxed for the first time all day.

"Did your wife and kids catch their plane on time? I know you were with the police for ages," I asked Hector.

"Yeah. Finally, I got the officer to understand they weren't even in Taos. And they have no knowledge of our business. They're back in L.A. now."

Greg set down his martini glass. "That's what surprised me most. The police questions—they were more about MedDyno than the skiing accident or events in Taos. But then, we learned they arrested Michael for something to do with the investigation into the business. I guess that's serious and progressing quickly?"

Hector paused for a moment. He picked up a spring roll from the plate we'd ordered for the table. After dipping it into the sauce and taking a bite, he cautiously responded. "Oh, it's serious, Greg."

Serious enough to kill someone over? Was Michael that desperate to hold onto the company? I thought, while watching Hector's body language as he explained what he knew about the pending lawsuits.

"They've confiscated all our files, all hard drives, laptops from every employee. Every single email *any* employee sent or received is being scrutinized." He picked up his beer and downed at least half of it, before signaling to the server he'd like another.

Greg finished a bite of the fried calamari appetizer. "From talking with Peter and Michael … heck, even Raj … I didn't realize it was so serious."

"You wouldn't have. None of them took it that way. Well, I know Raj is worried. But, all of them—they completely rely on their lawyers to get them out of every scrape."

"Have there been others?"

"Oh, I don't know … but this one has lingered around for a long time. Ever since I joined the company, actually."

"You don't seem concerned they'll arrest you. And, why Michael anyway? Do you know specifically what they are charging him with?"

"I am concerned, don't get me wrong. Everyone at the company needs to watch their step right now. I haven't purposely done anything wrong, mind you … however, I get the distinct feeling I'm going to be guilty by association. I've told them for a long time now to up their game related to the test trials. To take the accusations seriously and put all resources toward finding out if there's validity to them."

"And they didn't?" I asked.

"Not to the degree I would, if it were my company."

Our meals came, and the conversation slowed. Afterwards, we asked Hector what he thought about Peter's accident. A look crossed his face that I read as skeptical.

What he stated was, "I guess if the police deemed it an accident, then that's what it was."

"To our knowledge, the autopsy hasn't come back yet, so the 'official' cause of death isn't known, is it?" I asked.

"That's true. But, honestly, he was out in a wild country *on his own*. Lots of stuff can happen. That's another example of Peter's consequence thinking skills. He had none. Spontaneity is one thing, but he was reckless and rarely thought of the outcome."

"What do you think of Tammi hiring a hitman? Could that be how Peter died?"

We saw the look of shock in his expression. He hadn't heard about that theory. After collecting himself for a second, he asked, "I thought there wasn't evidence of bullets … gunshot injuries?"

"Doesn't mean the hitman used a gun … maybe poison instead?"

He chuckled. "Since when does a hired hitman use poison to kill their target?"

I agreed with him. Unless that hitman was a woman.

CHAPTER TWENTY-EIGHT

We arrived back at our hotel shortly after seven, slightly buzzed, and in much better spirits. Both of us were eager to get home finally. I missed my work. Greg didn't admit it, but I could see he was ready to get back to his as well.

Shadow was excited to see us and squirmed in her kennel. We took her for a leisurely stroll around the hotel property, then hunkered down in our warm suite. Greg turned on the TV; I put on a kettle for bedtime tea. My phone chimed, and I dug it out of my purse.

"Hmmm, Sam sent a message." I read it to Greg.

Sarah arrested for vandalism!

I was relieved that there would be accountability. I wondered why she did it, though. Seemed awfully petty for a woman of her age. I'd have thought that was the behavior of unthoughtful teenagers, not an adult.

Another message. **They will pick Tammi up in ABQ tonight—she was the other one in that footage**.

"So weird. Tammi is also being arrested for damaging Sam's place. Wasn't that the same day as Peter's disappearance?" I asked.

"Think so. But, at night, right?"

I nodded.

The kettle whistled, and I jumped, not remembering it had been heating. I poured a mug and then settled in on the sofa, cuddled next to Greg. Concentrating on a show was going to be difficult for me. I scrolled through social posts on my phone, mindlessly trying to detach from the day.

Another message came in—this time from Kelly.

Mom's here. Ana drew another picture!

A second later, an image displayed. In the center was the bakery, with shiny sparkling windows, and you could see gingerbread houses inside. So adorable. I still didn't understand how this kid was so talented. Then I remembered what they said about the spell book. *Could it possibly have helped her? Who knows?*

I zoomed in closer. My heart thumped.

"Hon, look."

The man's gaze never wavered. He was mesmerized by the reality TV show. I nudged him. "Greg. Look." I held up my phone.

Distractedly, he looked at the phone. "Uh, huh. Nice."

"No, please. Look … Ana drew this!"

"Looks like our hotel," he said, glancing back and forth at the TV.

"Exactly. HOW?"

"Hon, I don't know. But, you should see these guys … they're …" he pointed to the TV and busted out laughing.

I got off the couch and went upstairs to call Sam and Kelly. He obviously wasn't interested.

"Hey Kelly," I said, when she answered.

"Libby! Isn't it interesting how a new drawing shows the bakery all put back together? As though the universe has said, 'everything is right in the world again'," she chuckled.

"Yes, I love what Ana drew … the bakery, the gingerbread display." I hesitated, then mentioned, "Do you notice that other building in the background? The only thing that looks to be in a larger city?"

"Yeah. I wondered what that was, but Ana is always asking to go to the city, so I figured it was her fascination with that."

"Kelly, it's identical to where we are staying in Albuquerque. There's even a busy freeway exit near … so accurate! I don't know, after what happened earlier, I'm freaking out right now. I mean, what do Greg and I have to do with the drawing at this stage?"

"Oh. I see." I heard her shift attention to Sam and related the story. She put it on speakerphone.

Sam asked, "How'd the service go, Libby?"

"Yeah, everything went well. Sad, of course."

"Was Tammi there?"

"Oh yeah. Slandering Larry—er, Greg's brother—uh, another long story. Anyway, that was the last time I saw her."

"Well, we learned she was definitely with Sarah that night. Beau tells me she'll be brought in again for more questioning."

"Don't you find it strange that she and Sarah did not

hide from the cameras? I mean, yes, the footage was a little obscured, being nighttime and all. But they, themselves, made no attempt to cover their faces or even wear unassuming clothing. It's almost as though they *wanted* to get caught."

"I hadn't thought of that. Where're your thoughts going, Libby?" Kelly asked.

"I don't know; something still doesn't sit well with me. We've missed something and now with that picture you sent … well, it makes me feel I'm supposed to be doing more. The real criminals haven't been caught yet. There's more to the story, and we're supposed to figure it out."

"I don't know, Libby. Sounds like the police have things handled. Earlier, you mentioned the police had arrested Peter's business partner. That should wrap it up, right?"

"Yeah … I thought that earlier. But there's something still lingering. I don't know exactly what. Or, why."

Sam broke in, "Libby, you've had an eventful week. It's probably time to settle down. Enjoy your handsome man and travel safely back home tomorrow. We only wanted to share Ana's latest creation, so we'll let you get back to your evening."

We said goodbye again, and I went downstairs to find Shadow in my place on the couch, all nestled in with Greg. It was amusing to think how quickly she'd abandoned me for Greg, I chuckled to myself. I poured another cup of tea and joined them for a couple more hours before we crawled into bed.

CRASH!
Shadow barked.

I jolted awake. *What was that?* "Shadow, shush!"

Greg was snoring. *Of course, he was.*

I shook him awake.

"What?" he groaned.

Shadow whined, agitated.

"Shhhhh … someone's downstairs."

"What?" he whispered. "Here?"

"Shh…" I nodded, with my finger over my mouth. Each of us quietly moved our legs off the sides of the bed and stood. Tiptoeing, I softly walked over to Shadow's crate, which was set up in the corner of our room. I put my fingers through to comfort her. She was eager to get out and wouldn't stop whimpering.

Before opening it, I tried quieting her and listening for more sounds downstairs. Greg pulled on his pants.

He whispered, "I don't hear anything." His eyes moved frantically around the room, looking for something to use as a weapon. "Let her out—she'll chase off whatever it is."

I opened the crate, and sure enough, Shadow bolted downstairs, barking ferociously. Terrified she would get hurt, I chased after her.

"Libby!" Greg yelled, following the two of us.

We reached the bottom of the stairs. Our hotel room door was wide open. Shadow had run out. Thinking of the busy streets nearby—*the highway!* I panicked and ran. Greg grabbed his phone and called 9-1-1 while chasing after us.

I heard Shadow in the distance and ran toward her voice. Fear of the intruder was the last thing on my mind; I wanted to protect my dog. Rounding the corner of one building, headed toward the pool area, through the shadows, I saw a figure running and my girl was not far behind.

My lungs burned. I cringed with every barefoot step I took, but I never slowed down. Dodging branches from a tree and navigating around a flower bed, I ran directly toward Shadow's bark. Out onto the street, I saw them dodge behind an industrial looking building.

"Shadow!" I yelled. "Stop!" She didn't slow down at all. We really needed to work on commands.

On the other side of the industrial building was a major street. I panicked, pushing myself to run harder. "Shadow!"

Before they reached the street, Shadow jumped and knocked the person down. Her growling sounded nothing like my sweet baby. I caught up to them; Shadow stood over a slight figure with her snout right in their face.

"Get your dog off me!"

"Tammi?"

Shadow continued to growl.

"Get him off me!"

"Her," I corrected.

"Whatever!" she screeched.

Greg caught up to us by then. "Tammi?" he questioned.

He reached down as I pulled Shadow off Tammi. He helped Tammi up; I held tight to Shadow's collar. Tammi struggled to get away, so Greg used both arms wrapped around her tiny torso, holding her arms to her sides. Thankfully, Shadow settled and stayed right at my side.

"What were you doing in our hotel room?" I asked pointedly.

Greg got her settled down, and we started walking her back to the hotel.

"What they say about me isn't true!" she spat.

"What are *they* saying about you?" I asked. "Just tell us

what's going on…"

"I didn't hire anyone to kill Peter! That's ludicrous!"

We stepped off the street, back onto the hotel property. In the distance, I heard sirens. I knew we only had a few more minutes to get her to open up to us.

"Do you know why the police came up with that?"

She stopped. "Because my aunt did," she said solemnly.

Greg turned her around toward him. "Why would your aunt want to kill Peter? Did that have something to do with the insurance policy?"

"Oh, *please!*" she laughed. "Peter and I both had purchased large insurance policies before we married." Then she seemed to reconsider. She hung her head. "It's such a long story—my aunt. But, yes, I suppose she was all about money and status. The important part is that she never went through with it, okay? Yes, there's a paper trail, and it doesn't look good. I swear, she never carried it out once I learned about it."

I had Sarah's arrest in mind. Sam said Tammi was next. I wondered whether the charges were for more than the vandalism then. We prodded Tammi to continue walking.

"We know about the vandalism at that cute bakery in Taos. They captured you and Sarah on video doing it."

Her gaze dropped again. "Ok, so you do know who my aunt is. Yes, not my finest hour, for sure."

Greg asked, "So, I take it, that was also your aunt's idea?"

"She's disturbed … needs help. We've tried to get her help, but she's impossible."

We turned another corner and saw our building. Police surrounded it.

Hackles went up on Shadow's back and she barked. I held her tight.

"Guess it's time for you to confess everything to the police, Tammi. If you want your freedom," I said, as the officer's screamed for all of us to get to the ground. Guns were pointed directly our way.

Pulling Shadow closer to me with one hand, and showing the officers my other hand, we knelt to the ground and remained still. Greg and Tammi both lifted their arms in the air and crept to the ground at the same time.

A man walked over to where Shadow and I were on the ground. "Libby, you can get up now."

I looked up. "Hector?" He showed me his badge.

Several officers escorted Tammi into a squad car. Greg came over, extending his hand and helping me up. I kept staring at Hector in disbelief.

Hector was a cop?

CHAPTER TWENTY-NINE

Since nothing had gone to plan this far, it shouldn't have surprised me to learn that Hector was undercover the entire time.

We sat in the living room of our suite while the whole sordid story unraveled.

"Yes, that's correct," he answered Greg's question. "I've been on this case now for years. I was brought in by the FDA, when they initially began their investigation. As you already know, the authorities have suspected the company had cut corners along the way. Indeed, they had."

"Wow, that took a heck of a long time…" I muttered.

"You're telling me!" Hector scoffed.

Greg shook his head. "I'm so confused, though; what did you discover now that you couldn't prove from day one? Why did it take so long?"

"It's really complicated, Greg. I thought it would be an open and shut case, too. I had actually come to believe that MedDyno manufactured a perfectly safe device. Until the last person's death, about a year ago."

"What was different about that one?" I asked.

"There probably wasn't anything *different*, necessarily. But that's when I began collaborating with medical professionals who implant drug-delivery devices. I learned a lot."

He explained how he spent several months in that unit—reminding us of his scientific background and how he got the job at MedDyno to begin with. He had been at the top of his class at MIT. I wanted to ask how he became involved with the Feds, but that was for another time.

During his time assisting medical professionals, he continued to marvel at the invention Michael had developed. However, he also noticed shortcuts being taken. The doctors began complaining about how often certain parts failed. Everyone assured him that was not an issue, they had a great technical support team and would rush in any needed parts.

Greg added, "Raj told me how expensive the replacements were ... and how they began sourcing them cheaper; that's where they got themselves into trouble, right?"

"Wait, was Raj involved in that?" I asked.

He nodded. "He's the money man, remember?"

Greg hesitated, but asked anyway. "Peter and Michael knew substandard parts were being used? At the expense of other's lives?"

"Honestly, I think they were too far removed. But they also weren't innocent."

"Then, what does all this have to do with Michael's arrest?" I asked.

He cleared his throat. "Guys, new information came in tonight while we were at dinner. As soon as I left you, I met with the coroner, who conducted Peter's autopsy."

We leaned forward with anticipation.

"*Peter* proved the company's device was faulty," he stated matter-of-factly.

"Okay. *How?*" I was confused.

"That's how he died…"

Greg and I nearly fell out of our chairs. I stood, began pacing around.

"He was diabetic?"

"No. That's just it." Hector explained. "Apparently, he and Michael were bound and determined to prove investigators wrong. They took it upon themselves to conduct a highly illegal experiment—on Peter."

"Whoa! You've got to be kidding me!" Greg exclaimed.

"Long story short—the coroner discovered Peter had the implanted device. His insulin levels were off the charts. That's what killed him almost instantly."

"Why would he take insulin if he wasn't diabetic?" I asked, coming back to that subject.

"The way the device works—so long as your insulin levels were normal, the device would inject nothing. Peter apparently wanted to prove that it wasn't faulty. So long as it worked, he'd live a nice long life, diabetes or not."

I had to let that sink in.

"But, doesn't a doctor have to release the dosage … the device itself doesn't make that call? At least I think that's how I'd heard it explained earlier in the week."

Hector tapped his finger to his nose. "Precisely, Libby.

Michael faces murder, along with a host of other charges related to the coverup at his company."

I couldn't figure out what to say next. This was unbelievable.

Greg asked, "Wait, why Michael for murder? I get that it's his company, but if Peter willingly accepted the device to be implanted—how does that equate Michael to murder?"

"Well, like Libby said … a *person* has to administer the dosage. Since Peter and Michael were the only ones who knew about this, it stands to reason then that Michael administered it."

"But, why?" I asked. "If they were both out to prove their device was safe, why administer the dosage?"

"Because it *shouldn't have worked.* His insulin levels were fine."

"Is there an override to prevent mistakes like that? To stop the flow…" Greg asked.

"Yes. And he failed to activate it."

"Wow. I'm stunned," Greg uttered as he opened another beer. Once he sat down again, he asked, "Hector, Peter's father … the past couple days, his anger," he paused.

Hector knew exactly where Greg was going with the question.

"Greg, the man was so proud of his son, and Michael, whom he also viewed as a son. He thought the sun rose and set around those two. His unbecoming behavior is that of a grieving father." He shook his head in disbelief. "He was protective and fully stood behind them when their company came under attack. This news will kill him."

My heart broke for the Schulls.

"When you stayed at Peter's mountain house those

few days, did you notice the enormous safe room in their home?" I asked Hector.

"No, where was that?" His interest piqued, then he squinted at me. "Wait, how'd you know about it?"

I glossed over his second question and told him all about the hidden wall and several safes. Mainly, I was curious about what Peter was keeping so secure, but apparently, I wouldn't learn that information. I also told Hector about that word **memujidupe** I'd found on the notepad—in case it led to something that could help him with his investigation.

I divulged nothing about Kelly's daughter's drawings—that was information for us only.

CHAPTER THIRTY

The drive home from Albuquerque was uneventful. I left Greg in Heber at his house and drove the remaining two and a half hours on my own. I always felt sad when Greg and I parted, but that was life in a long-distance relationship. Certainly, after all the excitement of the past week, I rejoiced the second Shadow and I stepped inside our Mesa home.

Our roommate, Bella, greeted us briefly before heading off to class. I promised to update her on our adventures later. For now, a shower and a quiet evening alone with my pup were exactly what I needed.

By the next morning, I was refreshed and ready for a run. Shadow was too, by the look of things; she kept me at a pace I hadn't run since chasing Tammi down the road.

After a mile, we slowed and made our way back through the neighborhood to the spa. I purposely hadn't scheduled appointments for today, but I wanted to say hi to everyone.

Sitting in the Serenity room with a cup of tea, I filled Lexi in on what she'd missed after they'd left. She couldn't believe how convoluted everything turned out to be.

Lexi's head bobbed with some attitude, and she waved her finger back and forth. "So, you're telling me that unbeknownst to Tammi, her aunt Sarah actually looked into hiring someone to *kill* her new husband?"

"Uh, yeah. Only she didn't actually pull the trigger," I laughed, realizing my pun. "I mean, she didn't ultimately hire anyone. But she was stupid enough to have left a trail of her intentions."

"What kind of family are they? *Why* did she want to kill her niece's husband, anyway?"

"Apparently, greed—simple as that. She knew about the insurance policy and figured Tammi would take care of her, as she had done all those years after Tammi's parents died."

"I'm sure Tammi and Peter would have helped her out …"

"I'm not so sure about that. Tammi's still not high on my list. She was no saint, even though I felt for her losing her new husband so soon."

"Oh, oh, oh … what about Sarah's behavior at the bakery? The vandalism? Why?"

"She's a nutcase?" I laughed. "No, seriously, Hector told us what Tammi said about it. When Sarah realized Greg was in town for the wedding, she had this delusional idea that he and Tammi would get back together—like they were in high school. I guess her aunt had always tried to control her life and Tammi tried vigilantly to stay away from her. Anyway, Sarah wasn't happy to learn about the girlfriend Greg had brought to town. In fact, Tammi apparently admitted Sarah's plot to scare me back home the very first night we arrived in Albuquerque."

"You're kidding me." We both thought back to those bumps in the night I'd heard. "How would that have worked?"

"No idea. The woman is a loon. Well, you saw her behavior at the decorating contest … off her freaking rocker!" We both laughed.

"But Tammi was in love with Peter, right? She didn't share this notion with her aunt, did she?"

I shrugged. "I'll never know, but I don't think she agreed with her aunt. Anyway, she was playing around with Greg's brother by then anyway … so what does that actually say about her relationship with Peter?"

"No way!" Lexi hung her head. "It doesn't stop with her, does it?"

I laughed, because that was my point.

"So what now?" Lexi asked. "Michael is in jail. Tammi has some minor offenses—breaking into your room at the hotel, assisting in the bakery damage—yeah, what about that? *Why* did she help her aunt … what did they have against lovely Samantha Sweet?"

"It's going to be interesting to see how Michael fits in with Peter's death. It seems Peter agreed to the device implant—doesn't that make it suicide? I don't understand how Michael could be liable, and especially not for murder. However, it sounds as though the feds have a good case against the company—and the experiment those two conducted was highly unethical, if not illegal. I'm also sure that didn't help Michael out of his legal problems." I took another sip of my tea. Then, addressed her questions about the Sweets. "I can tell you what Kelly told me about her theory on the bakery's damage. She thinks Tammi got caught up in her aunt's stupidity. But she's also not ruling out a decades-long vendetta against those she felt ran her out of town. I have a different theory."

Lexi grinned. "What is it with small town vendettas? What's your theory?"

"I think Sarah got far enough down the path with the murder-for-hire plot she wanted an alibi. She also was considerate enough to involve Tammi, thereby giving her an alibi, too. There's also part of me that thinks she was vindictive enough to make Sam pay after not winning the contest."

"Oh, c'mon! She wouldn't have done all that over a stupid contest!"

I lifted my brows. "Wouldn't she?"

We laughed until our bellies hurt. It felt good. Then, we changed subjects and discussed our newly formed friendship with the Sweets. What lovely people they turned out to be. We both agreed our favorite parts of the vacation were those that included them. Kelly's Victorian-style home, that had haunted vibes, was incredible. Samantha and Beau's ranch home was stunning. But most of all, they were such a gracious family.

"It was so lovely how Sam and Beau included Joshua on their sleigh ride with their granddaughter!" Lexi exclaimed. "What a fun evening that was."

"What do you think about their magic boxes and that spell book?" I coaxed. "Oh! And Ana's drawing?"

Alexis got quiet. Then the twinkle in her eyes shined when she smiled at me. "I'm not sure I read into that as much as you did!"

"What do you mean? I wasn't 'all into it' … well," I considered, "it was kinda cool though, right?"

We both giggled. I honestly still wasn't sure about magic, or spell books, or whatever. Regardless, it was the best adventure I'd been on in a while—and that reminded me of Shadow's Christmas wish. We all got to spend time with the ones we loved, including discovering new friends.

Acknowledgements

My heartfelt thanks go out to several people …

Connie Shelton, I can't thank you enough for trusting me with your beloved characters. Ok, I won't lie—it freaked me out at moments, doing a crossover with a series as popular as the Samantha Sweet Mysteries, but I got there in the end! Your guidance over this past year has meant everything to me; thank you so much, Mom!

Ashley Quigley and Will De Wit, thank you so much for helping me over the hump with this story while I stayed with you in your beautiful home. Our impromptu brainstorming sessions over coffee stoked my creativity and got me going again. I finished it!!! I think both of you will easily recognize the bits you influenced. You are so loved and appreciated.

I truly appreciate my beta readers: Marcia Koopmann, Paula Webb, Susan Gross, Isobel Tamney, Dawn Hasiotis, and Eve Osborne. Each of you catch stuff in the manuscript that is impossible for me to see after I've worked for months on the story. Thank you, thank you, thank you!

And, as always, gratitude goes out to my beloved husband and four-legged babies (Libby, Bella, and Charley) who are there for me every day. I couldn't do it without you. I love you so much.

And to you, my readers! Thank you for taking the time to read *Shadow's Christmas Wish*. If you enjoyed it please tell your friends, and I would be so grateful if you would consider posting a review. Word of mouth is an author's best friend, and very much appreciated. Thank you!!

What's next for Libby and Shadow?
Libby and Shadow's next adventure is going to be something of a surprise! Subscribe to Jennifer's newsletter to be among the first to find out what happens next!
Don't miss Book 7 in this "impressively original and deftly crafted"* series! *Midwest Book Review*

* * *

Get another free book from Jennifer—Scan the QR code to find out how!

Books in the Libby Madsen Cozy Mysteries series:
Shadows in the Forest
Spa Shadows
Shadowed Treasures
Shadow Retreats
Spooky Shadows
Shadow's Christmas Wish
The Christmas Fairy – a holiday novella

Let's connect!
Website: www.jenniferjmorgan.com
Email: jennifer@jenniferjmorgan.com
Facebook: facebook.com/profile.
php?id=100076154359528
Twitter: twitter.com/JenniferJMorga3
BookBub: bookbub.com/profile/433830544
Goodreads: goodreads.com/user/show/148099219-
jennifer-morgan